I0725692

Return: Hansel and Gretel Retold

DEMELZA CARLTON

A tale in the Romance a Medieval Fairy Tale series

Lost Plot Press

ISBN-13: 978-1-925799-13-2

ISBN-10: 1-925799-13-1

DEDICATION

For all the other couples who've ever been mistaken
for brother and sister

One

"What about that plant? Can you tell me its properties?" Mother asked, pointing.

Rhona eyed the yellow flowers. "Tansy. Useful to combat gout or help a woman lose an unwanted child. We use it in tansy cakes and to scent the rushes on the floor on feast days."

"It can also be used to dye cloth in shades of yellow and green," Mother said.

Rhona sighed. "I will never remember them

all."

Mother turned and smiled. "Of course you will. One day. It takes practice, is all. There are books at home full of this, but your head needs to be full of it, too, for you won't have the book in the woods with you." She pointed at a plant with downy leaves. "What of that one?"

Rhona glared at the plant. "A stinging nettle. The young plants can be boiled and eaten, and the older ones can be soaked and the fibres woven into cloth. Best to wear gloves when you pick it, though." She had made that mistake once, and had no intention of doing so again. Nettles hurt.

"And that — " Mother gave a cry as her horse stumbled, and she tumbled from the saddle.

"Mother!"

Rhona slid from her horse and dashed to Mother. She lay face down, with a spreading pool of blood beneath her.

Rhona shook Mother's shoulder, and she'd never been so relieved to hear a groan in her life. "What should I do, Mother?" Rhona asked urgently.

"Use your magic, and get me home," Mother whispered.

"But you said…" Rhona snapped her mouth shut. She was old enough to know that her mother changed her mind when circumstances required it. "Very well."

Rhona took a deep breath, then bit her lip. The breeze came the instant she summoned it, plucking her clothing as it passed, but saving most of its power for Mother. She let the air currents lift Mother back onto her horse, but the animal shied as soon as it smelled blood. The frightened horse bolted, and Mother fell a second time.

This time, she didn't move.

Rhona sent another gust of wind, stronger this time, to pick Mother up and bring her to Rhona's own horse. Rhona's gelding was an old warhorse who shied at nothing, even as he was made to carry two women instead of one.

"Mother, should I go slowly, so I don't hurt you more, or should I hurry, to get you home faster?" Rhona asked.

No response.

That meant Mother wouldn't feel the jolting if they galloped, and they would arrive sooner. Rhona kneed her horse into flight, and the gelding willingly obeyed.

It was both the longest and the shortest ride of her life. Rhona shouted for help as she arrived at her father's house. Her arms ached from holding tight to her mother, but she refused to let go until Mother was in better hands than hers. Healer's hands, hopefully. Someone who knew how to stop the bleeding, for all Rhona's knowledge of herbs had fled when her mother fell.

"Rhona needs a healer, too!" someone shouted. Her oldest sister, Nuala.

Rhona shook her head irritably. "I'm fine. It's Mother who needs help."

"Why are you all covered in blood, then?" Nuala demanded with all the force of a twelve-year-old demanding to be considered a capable adult.

Rhona glanced down. The front of her dress was stained red. "Mother," she choked out, and ran for Mother's bedchamber. Nuala was hot on her heels.

Mother's eyes fluttered open. "Go get the other children, and your father," she said.

Rhona moved to obey, but Mother caught her sleeve. "No. Nuala, not you."

"I am sorry, mistress, but there is nothing more I can do. We can only wait," the healer said.

Mother nodded and waved the man out.

"I'm sorry. I should have gotten you here faster. I should have – " Rhona began.

Mother hushed her. "I do not have much time, he says. I lost too much blood. No one could save me, not even you. To think I'd hoped to give your father a son…but now I never will, and the babe will die with me. Just like my sister."

"Aunt Brigid – "

"Was no aunt to you, though she was my sister. She protected me as only she could, and so when she died, I swore to protect you. Now…it is your turn." Mother winced, then went on, "You must protect your sisters from whatever comes, but especially from Alban invaders. But you cannot use your powers, or they will know."

Rhona almost didn't want to ask, but she had to know. "Know what?"

"That I am not your mother. Brigid was."

"And my father…?"

"Is still your father. When the Albans attacked our home, I was already betrothed to him, his virgin bride, but the Albans…they…" Mother swallowed. "Brigid found me, too late to stop them. She swore she would protect me after that, but when it came to my own husband…the man I loved, I could not stand to have a man touch me. So she…pretended to be me, in the dark. We hid her pregnancy from your father and I told him you were mine. He does not know, and if he were ever to find out…I fear it would break his heart. He can never know you are a witch like Brigid. Never. But you must protect your sisters, like I protected you. Promise me!"

"Mother, I – "

"Promise me!"

Rhona fought to hold back her tears. "I swear on my father's life that I will protect my sisters."

Mother – no, Aunt Blanid – subsided.

"Thank you."

Then Sive, Maeve and Father arrived with Nuala, and all Blanid had time for were whispered words of love and farewell for her family before she left this world.

Then Rhona wept with her half-sisters, for they had all lost a mother that day, and life would never be the same again.

Two

"Tell us a story!" Sive demanded.

Nuala rolled her eyes at her youngest sister, but Rhona fought back tears. Blanid would have told her daughters a story to help them sleep, and Rhona had promised to take care of them.

Rhona moistened her lips. "How about the tale of the Three Little Pigs?"

Nuala gave the smallest nod, but Rhona caught it. This had always been Nuala's favourite.

"Once upon a time, there were three girls,"

Rhona began. "As alike as piglets, all born together, and none could tell them apart. Their mother had died when they were but babies, so a nurse cared for them. One day, when their father and all his household were busy preparing for a feast, the three sisters escaped into the woods, unseen. The nurse searched high and low, but could not find them anywhere. The girls had found a pond, hidden deep in the woods, where they began to play, not hearing the calls of their nurse or the other searchers. But it was a hot day, and a young wolf, separated from his pack, was thirsty, so he, too, was drawn to the pond to drink. And he found the three girls, playing in the mud. He snapped at one of them, but she was so covered in mud, she slipped free of his grasp, pulling her sisters deeper into the water where the wolf could not go. So the wolf, hungry and angry that his dinner had run away to where he could not reach it, set up such a howling that soon all those around heard it. Including the nurse, up at their father's house. When she heard that terrible sound, so close to the house, she thought of the girls. She took up a branch from one of the bonfires, and set off into the woods. She reached the pond, and when she saw the wolf on the edge, she beat him until she drove him off. Then she called the girls out of the water, but the frightened children wouldn't come. Finally, their father came, and the girls were dragged from the mud, looking more like pigs than human children, and forever after, they were known as the Three Little Pigs. Their father made them promise never to run away again, and the younger two agreed, but to this very day, the eldest has refused to give him her promise, and 'tis said that one day she will succeed her father as Lord of the Isles."

Maeve snorted. "That's not true. Girls can't be lords. She'll be a lady, and her husband will be the lord."

"She's already a lady. She doesn't need a husband for that," Nuala said, her eyes shining. This was why she loved the story so much, Rhona thought. Nuala had the true heart of a woman of the Isles, who would never be her husband's inferior. If she chose to marry at all.

"All girls must have husbands, Mother says.

To protect them," Sive said. Then her lip wobbled and her eyes filled with tears. "Mother!"

All three girls took up the wail, for they would never forget. Tonight the loss was fresh in their minds, and no story could soften that loss.

As Rhona's much longer arms wrapped around her sisters, she thought again of the Three Little Pigs. Three sisters, like the girls in her arms. Which made her the nurse with the stick, in accordance with Aunt Blanid's dying wish.

Rhona swore she would wield a mighty stick indeed, should any wolf seek to hurt her family. A blazing brand to set his fur on fire.

Three

The moment Grieve saw her, he knew he was in love.

Bedelia, Lord Calum's only daughter, a dark-haired girl ripe with curves in the all the right places. She blushed rosily as she offered a curtsey to Grieve and his older brother, Mahon.

Lord Lewis, their father, talked of marriage alliances and taking the girl on a tour of the island. Both brothers had heartily agreed to take Bedelia on the tour, and so it was settled.

Yet they had scarcely set out before a rider came galloping up to speak to Mahon on an urgent matter that simply would not wait. With a curse and an apology to Bedelia, Mahon turned his horse around and headed to where he was needed most. One day, he would succeed Lord Lewis as the lord of Myroy Isle, and he shouldered many of his father's duties in the meantime.

But that left Bedelia to Grieve, who thanked fate profusely, as he proceeded to show the girl the beauties of the northernmost of the Southern Isles. None of the views he presented to her compared to his own view, though — of the rosy cheeked maiden smiling at all she surveyed.

She spoke of her brothers, and how different life was at Langroy Isle, far to the south, so close to Alba you could see it across the water on a clear day. If Grieve sometimes lost track of her words, he blamed the lovely lilt of her voice, that turned his mind into a blissful fog of possibilities.

If he could persuade this girl to fall in love with him as readily as he'd fallen for her, the marriage alliance Father had spoken of would be more than just talk.

And he would have all those lovely curves in his bed…

Grieve daydreamed until dusk, when they returned home again, for the welcome feast Father had promised Bedelia.

She had the place of honour at Father's side, displacing Mahon, who sat between Bedelia and Grieve.

Grieve comforted himself with the thought that the next day, he would have her all to himself again, as they toured the western shores of Myroy, for Mahon would surely be called away for more important things again, leaving Bedelia and Grieve alone for love to blossom.

Father must have planned it this way, Grieve was certain of it.

Mahon was at least five years her senior, while Grieve was only a few months younger than Bedelia. Young for marriage, but not too young.

And Bedelia liked him, while she scarcely said a word to Mahon. Why, she could not even look at him for more than a moment. Whereas she'd shared plenty of smiles with Grieve while they rode together.

Yes, Grieve thought as he looked at her. Bedelia was his happily ever after, and nothing fate could do would change that.

Four

"Girls, I'd like you to meet my new wife and your new stepmother, Doireann. She has sworn to be a good mother to you girls, after your own was so cruelly taken from us." Father pushed the diminutive dark-haired woman forward. "Say hello."

Nuala, Sive and Maeve chorused their greetings, but Rhona merely nodded. She and her father had discussed the woman before he'd agreed to marry her. Doireann was a widow from Scitis Isle, whose husband had died defending their holding from Alban raiders. A fitting stepmother for her sisters, Father had said and Rhona had agreed, but Rhona had not realised she would be so young. Why, Doireann was only a few years older than Rhona herself.

Perhaps Father hoped to sire a son on the girl. As though she would want another child to care for while she was still busy with Nuala, Maeve and Sive. Sive was scarcely out of swaddling clothes, or so it seemed to Rhona.

"Perhaps you can all go berry picking in the woods tomorrow," Father suggested.

"They aren't ripe enough yet. In a week, would be better," Rhona said.

Father nodded sagely. "In a week, then. Doireann will be settled then, won't you?"

Doireann nodded obediently.

Overwhelmed by so much at once, Rhona guessed. She would be the same, if she married a lord who already had children.

Hope blossomed. Perhaps that was what Father had in mind. Giving the girls a stepmother, so that he might free Rhona herself for marriage. Not that she'd met a man she wanted yet, and Father would not press her into a marriage she did not want. No matter who her mother had been, Rhona was still a woman of the Southern Isles, a woman who chose her own fate and who she might marry.

Doireann was given chambers adjacent to the one Sive and Maeve shared. Not Blanid's room beside Father. She raised no complaint, and meekly did as she was bid. In fact, she said little or nothing, hardly daring to raise her eyes from the floor.

Maybe she was in mourning as much as Father was.

Rhona left her stepmother to her own devices and returned to her embroidery. She hated sewing with a passion, but someone had to teach Maeve, and Nuala would not. Nuala had claimed the dairy as her domain, for churning butter and cheesemaking were her favourite chores. Blanid had approved, and Rhona saw no need to interfere. She liked fresh butter and cheese as much as the next girl, though perhaps not as much as Sive liked drinking fresh cream. A habit Rhona had not yet managed to cure her of, though her stepmother might have more success.

Five

"You may go," Doireann said grandly to Ciara and Siobhan.

The two maids looked at each other, then Rhona.

"Return to your duties at the house, but leave the pony and the baskets," Doireann continued, growing impatient.

Berry picking was something the whole household did, from the lowest servant to the highest lady, or it had been for as long as Rhona could remember. They all ate their fill while filling their baskets, for berries were a summer treat that didn't last for long.

Remembering her father's admonition to make her stepmother feel welcome, Rhona forced a reassuring smile for the two girls. "I'll leave some for you to pick on the morrow, I promise. We shall manage. The girls are much bigger now, so they can carry a basket each." It would have to be a very small basket for Sive, or a very empty one, Rhona thought as she watched Maeve take Sive's hand to show her which berries to pick.

Nuala headed off on her own, swinging a large basket by her side as she selected the best looking bush.

Ciara and Siobhan mumbled something and headed home. Only then did Doireann take up a basket of her own. Ignoring the others, she proceeded to strip a bush on the far side of the clearing.

Rhona sighed and followed suit, only to find Doireann deliberately moving away from her, deeper into the forest, leaving her bushes half-picked. A quick glance told Rhona that her sisters were doing fine without her, so she followed Doireann. Deeper and deeper, until they were surrounded by trees and there wasn't a berry bush in sight.

"The berries are all back there," Rhona said, pointing.

Doireann waved away her words. "Let the children pick berries. I must find the holy spring. I know it's here. They say it was blessed by Saint Columba himself, and sprang up at his touch, and one cup will make any woman fertile, no matter how barren she may be. I heard Lady Catriona of Isla drank the miraculous waters of it on her wedding night, and that was the reason she gave birth to triplets."

Rhona shook her head. "I've never heard of such a spring. And Saint Columba didn't like women, so it does not seem likely he would work that sort of miracle. Especially not here. He feared the witch women of Nimbanmore."

Doireann scoffed, "There are no witches left in the world, least of all here. The faithful wiped such wicked creatures out centuries ago!"

Rhona wondered what the woman would say if she told her stepmother that magic was alive and well, coursing through her blood in readiness for when it was wanted, but she held her tongue. Blanid had told her to hide it, and hide it she would. No one must ever know.

"But the miraculous spring is real. It must be. I shall find it, and drink from it, so that I might bear Lord Ronin a son!" Doireann ducked between two trees, then trotted down a slope.

Rhona glanced back at her sisters. They were already out of sight. If she followed her stepmother, the girls would not know where they had gone. "Doireann, wait. The girls…"

"Go back to the children! I will find this spring on my own. It's not like you need it. You have no husband yet! Wait for me in the clearing. I shall not be long," Doireann called back before she disappeared from sight.

Rhona was torn. If something happened to her stepmother, her father would never forgive her. But if anything happened to her sisters…alone in the woods…Rhona would not forgive herself, and nor would Blanid. Wishing she didn't have to, Rhona said, "Very well. We shall wait."

Her dread-filled heart weighed more than her empty berry basket as Rhona returned to her sisters.

"Where is she?" Nuala asked, popping berries into her already stained mouth.

"Doireann has gone for a walk in the woods by herself. She wants us to wait here for her," Rhona said.

"More berries for us!" Sive cheered. Her hands and face were so covered in berry juice, she looked like she'd slaughtered a pig. Or a piglet, perhaps.

Rhona managed a smile for her sisters. "Let's see who can pick the most before she comes back."

Six

Twilight came, with no sign of Doireann. Rhona had spread a blanket upon the ground, and Sive lay on it, snoring softly. Maeve looked like she wanted to join her, and even Rhona longed for her bed. Nuala was determined to pick berries until the last of the light was gone, but that time was fast approaching.

Finally, Nuala plopped herself down beside Sive. "I wish I'd brought a cloak. I'm cold," she announced.

"I'd prefer a fire," Maeve said. "Much warmer."

Rhona could not magic a cloak into being, but she could build a fire. The warm day meant there was some tinder and a few sticks, but not much. A fallen tree held plenty of timber to burn in its broken branches, but Rhona had not thought to bring anything with which to light the fire.

Nevertheless, she piled up a collection of fuel, then crouched over it so she hid it from her sisters' sight. Only then did she dare bite her lip and unleash the most powerful part of her magic.

The log blazed to life, as though Rhona had added it to a roaring fireplace and not a cold nest of sticks.

Maeve clapped her hands. "Thank you, Rhona!" She stretched out her fingers to the blaze.

Darkness descended, leaving the four of them alone in the woods. Luckily the biggest beasts on Rum Isle were its cows – they would not have wolves to worry about, or bears. "We should probably huddle up together with the blanket by the fire to keep warm, while we wait for Doireann to return," she said. "I'm sure she'll see the light of it, if she is lost, and come back soon." This last was a lie, but her sisters did not need to know this. It was just another burden she would carry alone.

On the morrow, they would return home, and tell Father his wife was missing. He would send men out to search, and they would find her. Rum Isle was too small to hide her for long.

Rhona set several logs beside the campfire, so that she might add fuel through the night if she needed to, before joining her sisters in their blanket bower.

Nuala's eyes drooped, and she soon added her snores to Sive's. Maeve was still awake, though, and her watchful eyes regarded Rhona.

"Is she coming back?" Maeve whispered.

Rhona wet her lips. She didn't want to lie, but… "I hope so. Father would be heartbroken to lose another wife so soon after Mother's death."

An owl screeched in the distance, and Maeve squeaked like she'd been the owl's prey. "What is THAT?"

"Just an owl. You are too big for it to carry,

so it is nothing to worry about. It is catching mice."

Maeve shuffled closer to Rhona. "There are mice in the woods?" Her eyes were wide with terror.

Rhona smiled in the dark. She would never understand her sister's fear of the small creatures. "Not while the owls are out hunting. They are running to hide – probably in our barn."

"Good. Then the cat will get them. She has six kittens, you know." Maeve snuggled closer to Rhona. "Mother said you will protect us. It's true, isn't it? You will keep us safe?"

"As long as I draw breath, I will let nothing and no one hurt you, or any of my sisters," Rhona promised her, and every word rang with truth.

Using any means necessary, Rhona added in her head, as she threw another log on the fire. Even magical ones. No one hurt her family.

Seven

"The pony's gone!" Maeve cried.

Rhona winced at the rude awakening, wishing she could sleep a little longer in some place more comfortable. But she had to put on a brave face for her sisters. "I'm sure he's just gone to find some breakfast," she soothed. But there was plenty of grass in the clearing – grass he'd eagerly devoured yesterday. "Or he was thirsty."

That made more sense. "We should go down to the river for a wash and a drink, too, before we head home. Perhaps we shall find him there, and Doireann, too," Rhona continued, clambering to her feet.

The pony was indeed nowhere to be seen, along with the panniers of berries he'd been carrying. True to her word, Rhona had left some berries on the bushes, so there was enough for breakfast.

She helped Sive wash her breakfast berry juice from her face and hands, but when they still found no sign of the pony or Doireann, she had to admit defeat. "Fill your pockets with berries for on the way. Time to go home," Rhona said.

Eight

Rhona staggered up to the house, her arms aching from carrying Sive. What she wouldn't give to have the pony who'd carried Sive into the forest, but they'd seen no sign of the creature since last night. She tucked Sive into her bed, figuring the girl could wash when she woke in the morning. Maeve and Nuala had washed in the water butt outside, and were no doubt raiding the kitchen for dinner.

Rhona debated whether to join her sisters and grab a bite to eat, or head straight to bed and break her fast in the morning. Her stomach had churned with worry too much to allow her to eat today, and even now she wasn't sure if she could keep any food down. Not without knowing if Doireann was all right. Her father would never forgive her for losing his wife.

Though the hour was late, she should probably wake him to tell him the ill news. She padded softly to her father's chamber, and raised her fist to knock.

A distressed cry came from Sive's chamber. "Mama?"

Rhona's heart broke anew, and she turned to go to her sister.

"Rhona?"

Her father stood in the open doorway, looking distinctly displeased.

"I must see to Sive," Rhona said.

Father seized her arm. "Let Doireann do it."

To Rhona's surprise and relief, her stepmother emerged from her father's chamber, squeezed past them, and headed for Sive's room.

"So she made it back?" Rhona choked out.

Her father's brows lowered further. "No

thanks to you. What possessed you to take off like that, and with your sisters?"

Rhona was lost for words for a moment. Finally, she said, "I thought it would be safer…"

"Then you are a fool. A foolish child, who I thought was past such things. Really, Rhona? A miraculous spring blessed by Saint Columba himself? Where did you hear such nonsense?"

Rhona glanced at Sive's chamber, but Doireann had closed the door.

She did not want to make trouble for Doireann. "I do not remember, but I thought it strange that such a spring should exist so close to home, when I had not heard of it."

"Keeping your sisters out all night in search of this nonsense! What were you thinking?" Father demanded.

She hung her head. "I am sorry, Father. I lost track of the time. We should have returned before dark, but Sive was tired, and – "

"Enough! You are too young to take care of your sisters, no matter how mature your mother thought you might be. They are Doireann's responsibility, not yours. She told me she tried to dissuade you from finding this imaginary spring, especially when your sisters insisted upon following you, but you refused to listen and left without another word. What if one of you had been hurt, hmm? Doireann arrived after dark last night, quite distraught that you had not returned, though you had promised to be but a moment. You were gone hours, leaving her alone in woods she did not know!"

Rhona struggled to make sense of her father's words. No, it was Doireann who had set off to find the spring, who had told HER to wait, not the other way around. And her sisters had never left the clearing, except to wash by the river, and that was hardly but a step away from where they'd camped in the clearing.

"But, Father, I – " she began, not sure how to continue.

"I do not want to hear excuses, for nothing will excuse such reckless behaviour. Do you think any man will want a wife who puts the children under her care in danger, just to satisfy her own curiosity? Go to bed. On the morrow, you will beg your stepmother's forgiveness, and you will submit to whatever punishment she gives you. She is the lady of this house, and whatever she asks you to do, you will obey. Is that understood?"

Rhona swallowed back her fury. "Yes, Father," she lied.

"Good. We will not speak of this again, and hopefully the matter will be forgotten before rumours can spread outside our household. If Lord Lewis were to hear…but he shall not. Both Doireann and I will watch your behaviour carefully from now on, Rhona. So soon after losing your mother…I will not lose you girls as well!"

Seething, she made her way to her chamber and closed the door. She had not been sent to bed without dinner since before Nuala was born, and certainly never before when she had nothing wrong!

How had her father gotten the idea that she had gone searching for the stupid saint's spring? Rhona had not heard a whisper of the place until Doireann mentioned it.

Realisation dawned. Of course, Doireann

had reached home before her. Perhaps Doireann had expected them to have arrived already, and she'd been shocked to find the girls missing. Had she spun a story for her father, painting herself in a good light and placing the blame on Rhona?

Maeve might have made up such a story, but Rhona would never. Father had called Rhona childish, when it was his wife he should have been looking at. Why, the woman was not much older than Rhona, and if her father asked for the marriage to be annulled…perhaps the widow had nothing left, after the Alban raiders had taken everything from her.

Rhona's fury eased the tiniest bit. If she was faced with such a future, perhaps Rhona might lie. Perhaps. But that did not excuse Doireann. On the morrow, Rhona would not apologise to her stepmother. Instead, she would make sure the woman understood she knew what her stepmother was doing, and while she would forgive her the once, if Doireann ever blamed Rhona for her own faults again, Rhona would not be so lenient.

With that firm resolution uppermost in her mind, Rhona prepared for bed. It wasn't until she was tucked up in her blankets that her belly reminded her that she'd barely eaten all day. She rolled over onto her side, hoping to silence the grumbling sounds. She could eat her fill on the morrow, and every day thereafter. Rum Isle might not be the wealthiest of the isles, but they would never run short of food. Not while her father ruled the island.

Nine

After a week spent cleaning every inch of Blanid's former chamber twice, as Rhona's first effort hadn't met with her stepmother's approval, Rhona was ready to stuff the scrubbing brush down Doireann's throat and drown her with the bucket of dirty water.

One good thing had come of all this cleaning. Rhona had moved all of Blanid's things into her own chamber, though the haphazard jumble of chests made it difficult to reach her bed at the end of each exhausting day. Rhona promised herself she would go through everything and keep it safe for her sisters, but for now, she had to drag the mattress back to the bed from where she'd left it airing by the window.

Her arms ached as she made up the bed again, but Rhona had to admit a certain satisfaction at a job well done. The room was no longer Blanid's – if her spirit had lingered, it would not stay here. Even Blanid's favourite candlestick now sat on the table beside Rhona's bed – Doireann would not have it. But she would surely want some light, so Rhona headed down to the kitchen to see if a spare one could be found that was suitable for the new lady of the house.

It took some rummaging until she found a brass one so tarnished she barely recognised it for what it was, but when she carried it to the kitchen table, the cook exclaimed, "Why, I have not seen that since your grandmother died! 'Twas her favourite. Well I remember her coming down here when young Ronin could not sleep. She would sit the candle on that very table, cradle the boy in her arms, and sing him to sleep in that very chair. More often than not, I'd find her still there in the morning, fast asleep, when I came to light the morning fires. I was in my first year of service then."

Rhona blinked, trying to imagine Belen as a young maid, perhaps the same age as Nuala, and not the woman she'd known all her life. "I was looking for something suitable for Doireann." The old candleholder would not do for her stepmother, Rhona knew. Doireann would want the best, shiniest one in the house.

"And it will be, once it's had a polish," Belen said. "I'll get one of the girls to do it. Ciara!"

Ciara looked up from peeling the carrots. "Yes?"

"Polish that, will you? It's for her ladyship upstairs." Belen rolled her eyes heavenward.

Ciara didn't make the mistake of thinking that meant Rhona. "At least I can spit on that."

Rhona laughed. "I should probably clean that, too. She said I was to prepare the room myself, with no help from anyone else."

"You've done the work of two maids this week, and given both Ciara and Siobhan quite the holiday. 'Tis only fitting that she do this for you now, as is proper. The lady of the house should not rub her hands raw polishing some old brass." Belen gestured toward the chair where she'd said her father had fallen asleep in his mother's arms. "Rest a little, Lady Rhona."

Rhona smiled at the title. "I am no lady. Just my father's daughter on a good day, or a drudge on a bad one, like today."

"Not to us. Not to any of us. That slip of a girl might have married your father, but she is not Lady Blanid, or your lovely self. Lady Blanid ran this house, and indeed the whole isle, as smooth as the sea on a summer's day. She never came into the kitchen without a kind word for what was cooking, and a helping hand where it was needed. She never needed no titles to command respect. She was a lady, and so are you. That Doireann…she's as common as muck, and meddlesome besides. Why, she finds fault with every dish that comes out of this kitchen, though 'tis exactly what she ordered. She asks for less salt, so I spare the salt, and she complains 'tis too bland. I add more, and she complains 'tis inedible and sends the whole mess back to the kitchen. Well, let me tell you, that stew most certainly was not inedible. I had two helpings myself!" Belen grinned.

Resting while everyone else worked was not in Rhona's nature, so she picked up Ciara's knife and set to work on the carrots.

"You should hear her hold forth about the only way to chop carrots!" Belen continued.

Rhona faltered. "What way is that?"

"Never mind. I'm sure whatever you do will be good enough for everyone else, and more than good enough for her."

Rhona resumed peeling. Working with a knife was calming, much like preparing herbs in the stillroom, for the repetitive task allowed her mind to wander. But never far. Her thoughts turned to Blanid, or Brigid, or Doireann, and none of them were comforting right now.

Rhona said, "Belen, would you tell me a story, please? One of the folktales where the wicked are properly punished, and the ending is happy."

Belen tapped the spoon on the side of the stewpot. "My lady wishes for a tale? Lady Blanid was one for tales. We could swap them for hours – she knew more than me, for her family collected tales along with the plants they grew. Let me see…she used to tell this chilling tale of a brother and sister, lost in the woods.

"Once upon a time, there was a poor woodcutter and his wife who had two children, a boy and a girl, but they did not have the wherewithal to feed them. So one day, the father took the children into the woods with all the food they had, and left them there, hoping someone might take pity on the mites…"

Parents too poor to feed their children. That was something Rhona would never allow to happen on Rum Isle, she reflected, as she listened to the tale. Poor Hansel and Gretel would not have needed to take shelter with a wicked witch here.

By the time Belen's tale ended, the carrots were cut and Ciara stood beside Rhona, with her mouth open and the polished candlestick in her hand.

"Her ladyship will want the best beeswax candle for that. No tallow for her," Belen said, fitting a candle into the stick before handing it to Rhona. "When you're finished taking that up to her room, come back. I have a treat for you, and your sisters, if you choose to share it. One of the beekeepers brought some honey today, and he was so thankful for the poultice you made for his knee – which is quite healed, by the way – he brought you some honeycomb."

Now it was Rhona's turn to grin. "I will fly up those stairs, and back. You'll see!"

Up she went, but she slowed her steps as she heard voices. Specifically, her father's and Doireann's.

"I said no!" Her father sounded weary.

"But I need you in my bed, for 'tis not a proper marriage if it not consummated. You do want me, don't you, Ronin?" Doireann wheedled.

"I need you to take care of my daughters. My poor motherless girls."

"I could give you sons, if you but lie with me. Much better than girls."

"Watch your words, woman. I love my daughters, and if it were not for them, I would have left you to the charity of Scitis Isle. They need a mother, a woman to take care of them.

Rhona is too young, no matter what she may think. Besides, she will one day leave us to have her own children, and then what? Nay, take care of the children you have, woman, and leave me alone!" Father threw the door of Doireann's chamber open and stormed out.

Rhona ducked into the shadows, where no one would see her.

"But anything could happen to them. Like my family, taken from me in a single raid, and you will go from four girls to none. If you had more children, at least some would survive..." Doireann continued, reaching for Father. "Lie with me, Ronin. I promise I will bring you pleasure, and perhaps one day a son..."

"Lie with yourself!" He shook her off and shut the door to his chamber. Shutting her out.

Rhona felt a perverse pleasure at seeing her stepmother humiliated so, but if Doireann knew she had overheard...

"Anything could happen to them, Ronin. And when it does, then you will come to me. I swear it." Doireann's eyes glittered.

Rhona shivered, hugging the shadows even more fervently. If Doireann meant her and her sisters ill, then she would protect them any way she could. Doireann would not harm them. This Rhona swore, hoping the fire in her soul would hold her oath stronger than her stepmother's. For only one of them could win, and Rhona could not lose her sisters. Not now, not ever. And as for marriage? There was no way she'd leave her sisters at the mercy of her stepmother for some man.

Ten

Lord Lewis rose and the hall fell silent. "It is with great pleasure that I announce the betrothal of Lord Calum's daughter, the Lady Bedelia, to my son, Mahon."

What? Grieve tried to shout the word, but somehow before it left his throat his voice died.

Bedelia was to marry his brother? How?

The hall erupted in cheers and calls for more ale, so that they might drink to the health of the happy couple. Grieve drained his own wine cup, but his voice wasn't at the bottom of the cup, either.

He forced a smile as the toasts went on and on, until he finally found a chance to escape from the hell that the hall had become.

The moment he reached the yard outside, Grieve leaned against the wall, ready to throw up every bite he'd eaten. She was marrying Mahon? Why?

"Grieve!"

He thought he'd imagined her voice calling his name, but when he raised his head, there she was, haloed in the golden light spilling out of the hall. No, not a halo – hellfire, for that's what she was to him. Terrible temptation that would damn him forever.

He turned away.

"Why are you not happy for us? As my only friend here, I thought you would be the first to congratulate us, and wish us well."

Grieve moistened his lips. He prayed his voice had returned. "I thought we were friends, and maybe even more. But I was mistaken. We spent every day together, talking, laughing, as I showed you Myroy Isle, while my brother was too busy to spare even a moment for you. Yet you choose him, the brother you barely know, over me."

She drew herself up, dark eyes flashing. "I know he is the man I love, and the man I shall marry."

Grieve couldn't believe what he was hearing. "How can you love him? You've barely spent more than a moment in his company. It is those fairy stories you told me about – you have read too many of those, where a pair meet and fall in love in less than a moment. Such stories are not real!"

"I knew it the moment he kissed me," Bedelia insisted. "There was magic in his kiss. I felt it from my lips right down to the tips of my toes."

"You haven't been alone long enough with him for a kiss!" Grieve protested. "You've been with me every day! If I'd been forward enough…forgotten common courtesy…and stolen a kiss, would you have chosen me instead?"

He'd considered it, many times, but he'd always stopped himself. Now he regretted it more than ever.

"On my first night here, he asked if he might kiss me good night, to apologise for being absent from my side all day. His lips touched mine and…my heart was his." She stamped her foot. "He stole nothing I did not freely give. Not that first kiss, or anything after." A rosy blush coloured her cheeks.

Realisation dawned. Last night, Grieve thought he'd heard a woman's voice in Mahon's chambers. A maid or one of the girls from the village, he'd thought, and dismissed it. But it had been no maid. His brother had bedded the wanton Bedelia.

Grieve wasn't sure what came over him. Anger and bitterness and longing all collided and he couldn't think any more. He seized Bedelia's shoulders and pressed his lips to hers, desperate to show her how much he loved her.

She shoved him away, swiping a hand across her mouth.

"Your brother has more honour than you'll ever know," she snapped.

"Honour? What honour is there in taking you to his bed before you are married, treating you like a whore?"

Her hand landed on his cheek, a sharp sting from such a small hand. "I came to his chamber, to give him my answer to his proposal. I asked him to prove that he would be a good husband to me. This is still the Southern Isles, not Alba. A woman is free to choose, and I have. I chose well." She spat at his feet and stormed off.

"Bedelia, wait – "

Bedelia strode past a man whose face was in shadow. A man Grieve could not afford to ignore.

"Good night, Father," he said as he attempted to follow her.

Father caught his arm. "No, leave the girl. She will be your brother's wife soon enough, and you'll only make trouble for them. It seems you leave me no choice but to take you to the Council meeting with me, for I cannot leave you here."

Grieve hung his head. "She played me for a fool, Father."

The grip on Grieve's arm tightened. "No, you made a fool of yourself, son. Better men than you have made fools of themselves over women, and I'm sure you will not be the last. Better to learn wisdom, and not follow those who do not want you. Perhaps one day, a woman will invite you to her bed as readily as Bedelia did your brother. But until that day comes, stay away from your brother and his wife. Or I've no doubt she'll bruise your other cheek to match the one you'll have in the morning." Father laughed. "Pack your things. We leave on the morrow. Better to be early to this meeting, for I fear the Albans are preparing for war, and we must be ready when they come."

"I'll take war over women any day," Grieve muttered. Maybe he wouldn't need to marry at all. Not with Mahon and Bedelia rutting like rabbits. Why, they'd have a litter of heirs in no time.

Father only laughed. "Spoken like a man who knows little of either. But that will change."

Eleven

Father frowned over the message a breathless courier had just delivered. He'd run all the way from the harbour. "I must leave now – the Council meeting has been called early. The Alban king is looking at the Southern Isles again, and the raids are getting more and more brazen. Lord Angus and Lord Lewis believe it means war, which we must plan for." He seized Rhona's shoulders. "If you see boats coming, take Doireann and your sisters and hide. The caves will be well stocked, so you may hide there until my return."

Doireann hurried up. "What is this? What are you hiding?" She addressed Rhona, not Father, but it was Father who answered.

"Doireann, I must go to a Council meeting. If Alban raiders come as Lord Lewis says they will, you all must hide. Rhona knows the way." Father turned to go.

Doireann dug her claws into his arm. "You cannot leave me here with raiders on the way!" she screeched. "They will kill us all! I demand you take me to this hiding place at once!"

With difficulty, Father pried her off. "I do not have time. I must sail with the tide. Rhona will take you there, if it becomes necessary." He headed upstairs to pack.

Doireann followed him, her loud protests and pleadings audible to everyone in the household. Rhona pitied the woman, who had every right to fear a raid, for she had lost everything in one before. But Scitis was a barren rock, nothing like Rum Isle. Rum Isle protected its own.

Finally, Father departed, riding off at a gallop before Doireann got the idea in her head to go after him.

Doireann fumed for a moment, before she turned her fury on Rhona. "Take me to this safe place. Now!" She dug her fingers into Rhona's arm, much like she'd done with Father.

Rhona looked deep into the crazed woman's eyes, and saw something other than fear. Desperation, perhaps? She did not know. But she would not stand for being manhandled by this woman. Fury burned deep within her, and it was almost like Doireann felt it, for she released Rhona with a hiss of pain.

"If you insist, I will take you to Sanctuary in the morning. It is a day's journey, for we can only ride so far, before we must proceed on foot. But we will never find it in the dark." Rhona turned and headed back to the stillroom.

To her relief, Doireann did not follow.

Twelve

Grieve stayed on the shore of Loch Findlugan among the other lords' sons and retainers. Servants busied themselves with preparing tents and food for their lords, but like the other sons, Grieve had little to do.

Not for the first time, he wondered why his father had bothered to bring him to the meeting, if there was nothing for him to do. Only the lords of the isles were allowed on Council Island.

Father should have left him at home. Bedelia had been sent back to her father's house to prepare dresses and such things for her wedding to Mahon, so it wasn't like Grieve would have been in the way at home. Maybe Grieve shouldn't have mentioned his desire to challenge Mahon for Bedelia. But what else did a man do when his brother had stolen the affections of the woman he loved?

The familiar thwack of metal finding its mark roused Grieve from his dark thoughts. He'd always enjoyed archery – so much so that his father had allowed him to train some of the other local men to hit a target. If the Albans invaded, it would be by sea, and every arrow that found its mark before the Albans reached shore meant one less man to fight.

Laughter greeted Grieve as he joined the men assembled in front of the target. He soon saw why.

"Has a witch cast a spell on the target so that no one can hit it?" he asked.

More laughter. Someone handed the bow to Grieve. "Let's see if you can do better."

They backed up, allowing him space to line up his shot. An unfamiliar bow, when he'd been too busy riding with Bedelia or sailing to practice…Grieve would be lucky to hit the target at all. Yet he refused to back down from the challenge. Notch, draw, breathe…release.

His arrow thwacked into the target, slightly left of the centre.

A smattering of applause broke out.

"Who's next?" Grieve asked, holding out the bow.

Someone snatched it from his hand, muttering that they could do better.

The man beside Grieve stuck out his hand. "I'm Damhan. Lord Roe's son."

Grieve shook his hand. "Grieve. I'm Lord Lewis's."

"Are you the one Bedelia's going to marry? She's fallen hard for you. Singing and hugging herself and talking of nothing but going home to Myroy," another man said, eyeing Grieve with interest. "I'm Dermot. Lord Calum's my father."

Grieve hung his head. "No, she's to marry my older brother."

Dermot grinned. "Lucky escape for you, then. She's Father's little princess, leading him around like he had a ring through his nose.

She'll do the same for your poor brother, I've no doubt. You're better off finding a girl more biddable, or one who has no brothers, and a claim to an island that'll come to you when you marry. They say one of Lord Angus's three daughters will inherit Isla."

"You mean the Three Little Pigs?" Grieve blurted out. Everyone had heard the tales of the girls, who must be homely as hell to have kept such a terrible name.

Damhan waved his hand, as if dispelling an unwelcome odour. "Ah, they only got called that for the day they played in the mud. Comely girls, all three of them, with their mother's red hair. Though with a dowry like Isla, none of them need to be more than tolerable. I'd court any of them, if they looked my way."

"My father says Isla had best be held by a Viken after Angus, and he's keeping the oldest girl for an alliance with the Viken king."

The bow had come back to Grieve, and he took his turn. His second shot was better than the first — and much better than any of the others.

"She's still a woman of the Southern Isles, or she will be, if she's too young to be a woman yet. No Viken will have Lord Angus' daughter against her will while a single Islander draws breath. If she falls in love with an Islander, she'll marry where she pleases. Much like her mother did, to my father's endless sorrow," Dermot said, drawing back the bow. His shot landed in the dirt three feet in front of the target.

"Try again," Grieve urged him. "Only this time, aim a yard higher. The arrow will naturally fall to earth, so you need to let it soar more first."

Dermot nodded, and did as Grieve suggested. A moment later, his arrow thwacked solidly into the centre circle of the target.

More applause and a couple of cheers.

"Who's next?" Dermot asked, lifting the bow up in invitation.

"Me," said a boy. "But only if Grieve here can offer me some coaching. So that next time I shoot an Alban, I hit him right between the eyes instead of between the legs."

Laughter erupted, and cries of, "There's nothing to hit between an Alban's legs, anyway!"

Grieve grinned. Maybe Father had been right to bring him along after all.

Thirteen

Rhona did not sleep well, so she slipped into the stillroom for some willow bark to ease her headache on her way to breakfast. Dealing with Doireann and a headache was more than any saint could be expected to endure, and Rhona was certainly no saint.

Yet as she entered, she had the distinct feeling that something was wrong. The drawers were not all closed properly, and she made a particular point of shutting her jars away from all light so that the herbs might keep for longer. The books were out of order, too – Blanid's carefully drawn herbals, listing every plant she'd ever heard of, and quite a few that Rhona knew would never grow on Rum Isle. Rhona knew them by heart, of course, but occasionally she still checked some of the more exotic ones before administering them to anyone. She didn't know how her grandparents had procured some of the plants they possessed, but they'd made sure Blanid's stillroom held everything their own garden could supply.

"Lady Rhona, her ladyship demands to know when you are ready," Ciara said.

After Belen took up the title, they'd all started doing it, and Rhona could not bring herself to tell them to stop. They didn't look at her differently, nor curtsey at her like she was some princess, but now they came to her as they must have once come to Blanid. The message was clear – the staff saw Rhona as the lady of the house, not Doireann. It earned her more of Doireann's dark looks, even as it lessened the weight of her father's disappointment, just a little, but not enough to make her feel safe in her own home again.

And now someone had been through her herbs – since she'd left the stillroom last night.

"Ciara, did you or any of the others come in here last night, or this morning? Perhaps to get some willow bark, or herbs for cooking?"

Ciara shook her head. "Not me, mistress. I wouldn't know one herb from the other."

"But the herbs are all in my books, and I was still abed. You or one of the others might have opened one of the herbals to read…" Rhona stopped when she realised Ciara has trying to smother a laugh. "What is it?"

"You forget, Lady Rhona, that the only ladies who can read in the house are you and your sisters. Unless it was a matter of life or death, we would all let you sleep, and ask you for what was needed when you woke."

Of course. No wonder the girl laughed. Her sisters would wake her if they wanted something, knowing they would have it faster from her than from a lot of tiresome reading. "What of Doireann?" Rhona asked urgently.

Ciara shrugged. "I do not know. But surely she would summon you if she wanted something…"

Unless Doireann wanted something she did not want Rhona to know about. Medicines could be poisons if used in the wrong dosage, as Rhona knew well.

"Have my sisters come down for breakfast?" Rhona asked.

"Yes. Her ladyship insisted. Then she asked for some small cups so that they could all drink a special cordial…"

Rhona swore. Whether by design or mistake, Doireann might have poisoned the girls already. "Tell her I'm coming." She rummaged through the bottles, but she couldn't be sure which one Doireann had taken. Unlike the cupboards, the bottles appeared untouched. Everything seemed to be there, unless Doireann had poured the contents of one into a bottle of her own. And Rhona wouldn't know which bottle to check — it wasn't like she kept track of how much was in each one. Blanid might have known, but she wasn't here now.

Rhona paused to grab a cloak before heading outside, where Doireann sat on the box seat of a cart. A cart full of chests and casks, which were occupied by her bleary-eyed sisters. Sleepy from being woken too early, or because they'd been drugged?

Please, don't let it be the second, Rhona prayed silently as she approached the cart. "It will take longer by cart," Rhona said.

"I am not leaving my things here to be stolen by raiders. Show me to the place where we will be safe!" Doireann insisted.

Reluctantly, Rhona climbed onto the cart beside her sisters and they set off down the road, or what passed for one on Rum Isle.

"Which way?" Doireann demanded every time they reached a fork where the cart tracks went more than one way.

Rhona would respond with right or left or to continue straight, until she felt as drowsy as her sisters in the summer heat. She'd brought a cloak, but perhaps she should have thought to bring a hat.

"I'm thirsty," Sive announced.

Before Rhona could stop her, Maeve uncorked a flask and held it to her sister's lips. Sive gulped the liquid down, her eyelids drooping, before she slid off her box and lay down on the bottom of the cart, sound asleep. Beside Nuala, Rhona realised in horror. Then Maeve picked up the flask and drained the contents. She toppled to the floor, too.

Rhona snatched the flask from Maeve's slack fingers. "What did you give them?" She inhaled deeply at the lip of the bottle, trying to discern the contents. Strong spirits burned the inside of her nostrils, softened by the scent of lavender. That couldn't be all she'd given them. Some poisons had no odour, but one could taste them…

"Just a draught to put them to sleep, so that they will stay quiet. Now, tell me where Rum Isle hides its riches, and nothing worse will happen to them," Doireann said, her eyes flashing.

"Rum Isle's secrets are known only to its own. You may have married my father, but you will never be one of us," Rhona spat. She tipped up the flask and let a drop of the treacherous liquor fall onto her tongue. Spirit burn and lavender sweetness, without the one thing Rhona dreaded – the bitter gall of opium from the Holy Land. Perhaps Doireann had not found it yet. As it was, the liquor was a strong sleeping potion, no more, that would leave the user with a hangover and headache when they awoke, at worst. She let the flask slip from her fingers.

Just in time to see something dark blot out the sun before it collided with her head, and all the lights went out.

Fourteen

It seemed almost no time at all before the final
feast was over and the Council dispersed to go
home. Grieve rode with Dermot, Damhan and
the boy whose name was Brian, while his
father lagged behind, discussing serious
matters with Lord Ronin. At least, they looked
serious – Father could be discussing a chess
match with the man, for all Grieve knew.

Ships lined up in the harbour, waiting for
the tide to take them all home.

Grieve made to follow Father to their
vessel, but Father shook his head. "You're to

go with Lord Ronin. He needs an archery instructor for his men, as he has no sons of his own. Albans will strike at Rum Isle before they make it to Myroy, you may be sure, so it behoves the lords of the inner isles to keep up their defences to give the rest of us warning in the event they send more than a raiding party."

Lord Ronin inclined his head. "Your father tells me you have the makings of a good master-at-arms, young Grieve, and some skills with a bow."

Grieve lifted his chin proudly. "I have trained my father's men since I came to manhood, Lord Ronin, and I was easily the best archer among the boys on shore today. But with practice, they might be able to match my skill."

Father laughed. "He'll never be good at chess, like I told you. Too forthright for playing at politics. But I hope he will be just the man you need, Ronin." He gave the command for his crew to raise the sail and was soon out in the bay, out of earshot.

No word of farewell, or when Grieve might be allowed to come home. Maybe never.

Lord Ronin eyed Grieve. "We shall see. Come, boy. You're too old to be a proper page or fosterling, but still young enough that I can call you my squire. Master-at-arms and other such offices can wait until you've had time to prove yourself."

"Yes, my lord. And I will," Grieve swore.

Lord Ronin smiled. "Good man. Climb aboard." He gestured toward his boat.

For a moment, Grieve was lost. An unproven boy, a new squire, a good man...what was he really? He had no home, and no family around him any more.

Time to choose his own fate. Grieve strode aboard the ship bound for Rum Isle, vowing to show Lord Ronin, his father and any other man with eyes to see that he would prove he was every bit as good as his brother. Better, maybe. And Bedelia? She could be miserable with Mahon, for Grieve would not give the girl another thought.

Fifteen

The bright summer's day had given way to miserable weather, but the rain pattering on the ground was nothing to the drumming inside Rhona's head. Rhona groaned, sat up, then groaned again.

"Where are we?" Nuala asked.

Rhona blinked. Her sisters huddled together under a pine tree. Of course, they hadn't thought to drag her under shelter, too. Then again, if they'd drunk enough strong spirits to send them to sleep, they wouldn't feel much better than she did right now. In no shape to be dragging anyone's body.

"Not at home, where we should be," Rhona grumbled. She shuffled under the tree with her sisters. Only now did she realise fog had crept over the island, as it did on days like this. They could be spitting distance from home, and she would not be able to see it.

Rhona bit her lip, hoping to stir up a breeze to improve visibility.

"I'm cold!" Sive moaned, climbing into Nuala's lap.

Rhona let the breeze swirl away into the woods. Yes, the fog lifted just enough to show the tree trunks before it was all whiteness once more. They could not be far from the edge, if Doireann had dumped them from the cart. She would not have had the strength to drag Rhona far from the road, unless she'd had help.

But who on Rum Isle would help Doireann against Lord Ronin's children? No one Rhona knew. And as the mistress of Blanid's stillroom, she knew everyone on the island.

"We must wait for the fog to clear, and then we will find shelter from the rain. I'm sure there is a cottage or croft quite close, but we might miss it in the mist. Once we know where we are, we can go home," Rhona promised.

"Can you tell us a story to pass the time?" Maeve asked.

"The Three Little Pigs?"

Maeve shook her head. "Something else. Something new. We have heard that tale too many times."

And there would be no nurse come to save them today, Rhona knew. It would be up to her and her sisters to find their way home. She thought of the tale Belen had told her, the first night she'd called her Lady Rhona. That might do. "Have you heard the tale of Hansel and Gretel?"

The girls shook their heads.

Rhona drew in a deep breath. "Once upon a time…"

Sixteen

Grieve eyed the huddle of buildings on the clifftop as they approached Rum Island. "You'll need better fortifications than that," he observed. "Plus a barracks hall or two to accommodate your people if you are invaded. Father had me build a new hall at the beginning of this year, so we'd be able to house the women and children, not just the menfolk."

Lord Ronin laughed. "Rum Isle may be closer to Alba, but we are not as numerous as the people of Myroy or Isla. I think you'll find we have shelter enough for all of us, but the fortifications are not a bad idea. When we get the island men assembled, we can discuss it then." He nodded at the house. "First, I must greet my family, for they'll have missed me."

Butterflies rioted in Grieve's belly. Lord Ronin had spoken affectionately of his wife and daughters, but meeting them was another thing entirely. What if they did not like him? He managed with strange men and boys just fine, but girls? Bedelia was the only one he'd shared a house with since his mother had died, and he didn't want to remember how badly that had gone.

"This is Doireann, my wife," Lord Ronin said, wrapping an arm around a woman who resembled Bedelia. Well, small and dark, at least — she was thinner, without the luscious curves that had attracted him to Bedelia. And Doireann did not smile.

"Where are the girls?" Lord Ronin asked her.

Doireann's frown deepened. "I must speak to you about them. The oldest one, she turns the others against me. Not three days ago, they disappeared, and I could find no trace of them. I have not seen…"

"Father!" The same word cried by three different voices, as three girls raced along the path to embrace Lord Ronin.

The three girls looked like they'd been playing in the woods, judging by their muddied clothing and the twigs and leaves that clung to them.

Their mother looked like she was building up to give them a good scolding. One Grieve did not intend to witness.

"I'll go see about some timber to start those fortifications, shall I?" he said to no one in particular, and headed off in search of an axe.

Seventeen

They'd seen Father's ship arrive in the harbour, and hurried to get to the house before he did. Alas, they'd been too slow.

Doireann and Father stood outside the house, at a distance where no one could stand close enough to overhear them without being seen.

At least, no one who did not have magical means of hearing.

Rhona bit her lip, letting a little of her magic out to create a breeze that brought back the sound of Father's conversation with Doireann.

As she suspected, the woman was telling lies again.

"You girls run ahead. Father is home," she said to her sisters.

Nuala and Maeve seized Sive's hands and took off up the hill, shouting Father's name.

Rhona longed to run with them, but it was more important to make sure Candace arrived safely. The old woman had grown an alarming shade of pink as she huffed and puffed her way up the hill. Still, she waved away Rhona's offer of assistance.

"If I cannot walk up this hill under my own power, how will I ever run around after those three little fillies? Nay, if you are as spry when you are my age, girl, then you will thank the heavens yourself." Candace grinned and continued ambling, ever upward.

"You must not let them eat or drink anything she has touched. Nor let her touch them, either," Rhona said. "She tried to poison us once. There is no knowing what else that witch will try next."

"It's been a long time since there's been a witch at Rum Isle, or any of the Southern

Isles," Candace said, shooting a sideways glance at Rhona. "Not since your aunt, Brigid, died. But she was a good witch, always willing to help. Perhaps this one is not as experienced, and gave the children the wrong dose or the wrong herb. She is young, you said, not much older than you."

Rhona tossed her head. "I would not make such a mistake. Mother taught me better than that." No, Aunt Blanid, she corrected in her head.

When they reached the house, Doireann had left, and Father stood alone.

"Widow Candace," Father greeted her, before offering Rhona a kiss. "It is a long walk from your cottage. What brings you here?"

"Doireann poisoned us, then left us in the woods," Rhona snapped. "I managed to get the girls to Candace's cottage, but Maeve took a chill, so we stayed a little until she recovered enough to walk home. Candace has agreed to come and help take care of the girls, as their nurse."

Father blinked. "I'm sure it is all a mistake. She's such a sweet girl, she would never…" He shook his head. "I apologise, Widow Candace, for the stories my daughter has been filling your head with. I shall send you home on horseback, with gifts from my cellar to repay you for your time."

"My cottage is cold now my daughters are all married. Seems I could be useful here, if your daughters are giving you trouble," Candace said.

Rhona opened her mouth to protest, but a hard look from Candace silenced her.

"Your new wife is just finding her feet, after all. I'm sure I shall be a great help to her. I am used to work, and the lady of Rum Isle has enough cares resting on her shoulders." Candace moved toward the house. "I shall start by seeing those girls wash up. They look a fright, after walking in the woods. You'll see. I'll take good care of them." This last earned Rhona another look from Candace before she vanished inside.

Whatever Candace believed, at least she would watch over her sisters. Rhona couldn't ask for much more than that.

"I must speak to Doireann," Father said.

When Rhona stepped forward to follow him, he held up his hand. "Alone, Rhona. I will speak to you later."

Damn right, he would. And she'd have just as much to say. In the meantime, Candace would keep an eye on the girls, while Rhona changed out of her soiled gown. Something brighter and cleaner was needed, as befitted a dinner that would double as her father's welcome home after the Council meeting. Ugh, and a clean shift. One that didn't have leaves in it, or mudstains in places where no mud should be.

Rhona marched toward her chamber, intent on making herself presentable once more.

There was still some water in the jug, so she stripped off and washed. The fresh shift clung to her still-damp skin, letting off a faint whiff of lavender. The shift had not lain in the chest long, then – those in the bottom would smell much stronger.

She reached for the blue gown she'd worn at the last feast day, when Mother – Blanid – had presided over the feast with all the joy of a woman who'd had no idea it would be her last celebration. Blanid had clucked over the gown that day, telling Rhona she needed to wear more womanly things, for the hem of the gown that had been suitable for the girl Rhona had been was far too high for the woman she had now become.

The dress fell from Rhona's nerveless fingers back into the chest. She should give it to Nuala, but then what would Rhona wear? Blanid had promised to make her new gowns that fit her better, but she'd died before she could even cut the cloth, and Rhona was no seamstress.

The only womanly gowns Blanid had left had been her own. Gowns that would be wasted on Doireann, who had no right to wear them, either, Rhona fumed.

For the first time since Blanid had died, Rhona knelt beside the chests she'd moved from Blanid's chamber to her own. She opened the first, and breathed in the rose scent that Blanid had made wholly her own. Not least because her precious roses, which were carefully tended in the sheltered southern herb garden, had come with her to the island when she'd married Father. Other women had dowries of cloth and jewels, lands and houses, but Blanid and Brigid's parents had been renowned for their glorious garden, modelled on the one where Rhona's grandmother had grown up. So it was no surprise that Blanid had arrived with as many medicinal plants as her parents could provide.

Or had that been Brigid's doing?

Rhona would never know, now, for the two women who might have told her were now dead, silenced forever.

But with them both gone, she had a responsibility to remind her father who ruled here. And it wasn't Doireann, the conniving widow from Scitis.

Rhona dug through the dresses, looking for the sky-blue gown Blanid had worn which matched her own. Instead, she found one of yellow-gold silk, so soft to the touch she'd lifted it out of the chest before she knew what she was doing. It was lined with cream lambswool, as soft inside as out. Rhona had never seen Blanid wear this gown, yet when Rhona pressed her face to the fabric, she smelled an unfamiliar scent – sharp and fresh, tingling her nostrils as though it was something she should remember, but had forgotten. Citron, was that was this was called? No, the word was lemon. A kind of fruit that grew in warmer climes than here.

In her grandparents' garden, most likely.

Rhona slipped the gown over her head, letting the lambswool embrace her like it had been made for her. Only her waist was narrower, so she tightened the laces a little before tying them again. Blanid's bronze mirror stood in the corner, polished to a high sheen so that Rhona might see how well she looked. Or how well she might look, if she picked the bird's nest remnants out of her hair.

Swearing, Rhona unbound her hair and found a comb. It would take some time to get all the twigs and leaves out, but she would need to if she wanted to remind Father that she was a woman grown, and every bit as worthy as Doireann of being believed.

When she had finally freed her hair of snarls, tangles and twigs, she had to decide whether to pin it up, or leave it loose. Loose would attract more leaves the moment she ventured into the woods again, but that's how Blanid had worn hers at every feast day. A few pins, or a headband fashioned from a pair of narrow braids, were all that restrained the golden mane Blanid had proudly worn loose as she presided over the people of Rum Island.

The thwack of an axe hitting wood reached Rhona's ears. She peered out the window, wondering why anyone would be chopping wood so late in the day. They had cut turf enough to feed the house fires well into next month – no one should be cutting precious timber.

But there was no one at the chopping block, and besides, the sound was coming from down by the river. The only timber by the river was the willow trees, bred from the one that had been part of Blanid's dowry. The only source of willow bark on the island. If anyone was cutting into those trees, they'd have her to answer to. Especially if they wasted any of that precious bark.

Rhona slid a pair of boots onto her feet and marched out for confrontation.

Eighteen

"What in heaven's name are you doing?"

The voice was feminine, but authoritative. Accustomed to being obeyed. It could only belong to Lord Ronin's wife, Lady Doireann. Grieve let the axe hang by his side, no threat to the lady. "My lady, Lord Ronin wishes to build better fortifications to protect your house and all those who live there." He lifted the axe for another swing.

"Touch that tree again, and I promise you shall regret it. Even more so when I refused to give you any willow bark for the pain."

Grieve whirled, shocked. Lady Doireann had looked so small and docile – not the sort of woman who would threaten him with pain for touching a tree, of all things. "M-my lady?" he stammered.

He glimpsed the tall figure coming toward him, before the sun chose its own moment to enter the fray. The rays blinded him, and appeared to set fire to her. One moment a woman, the next a golden pillar of flame, heading inexorably for him. The axe dropped from his nerveless fingers. Grieve wanted to run, but at the same time, he didn't dare take his eyes off the terrifying spectre before him.

"What is wrong with you, boy?" she demanded.

As if to make his mortification complete, the sun hid its face behind a cloud once more. The fiery goddess transformed into a woman. A woman who didn't look a bit like Lady Doireann. Wheat coloured curls hung to her waist. The breeze played with some of the outer tendrils, the movement reminiscent of tongues of fire. Add that to the butter-coloured dress she wore, and it was easy to see how his overactive imagination had turned a girl into a goddess, with just a bit of sunlight.

He laughed shakily. "For a moment, I thought you were on fire," he admitted. He traced the shape of her body in the air. "Sunlight in your hair and in your dress. It looked like you were wreathed in flames. I thought I was going to die, and that you were going to burn me to death, without the flames touching you at all."

She backed up a step, her eyes widening in horror. She almost tripped over the hem of her gown, which was a little long for her, he'd only just noticed. She cast her eyes down. "My mother told me many times not to play with fire."

Grieve managed a smile. "My mother told me the same thing," he said. "But I did not listen. I once burned down a whole hay shed. My brother told me the cat had had a litter of kittens and that I could see them in the morning, but I was impatient, and took a candle in there at night..." Now it was Grieve's turn to bow his head. "I earned a sound thrashing from my father for that, and as a punishment he made me rebuild the hay shed. After that, I preferred to build with wood, not set fire to it."

Her eyes was still wide. "And what of the kittens?" Her voice trembled. She might look like a woman but she could not be much older than Grieve himself.

Now Grieve grinned. "They were never in the hay shed. The cat had her kittens in the barn, where the dairy cows slept." He held out a tentative hand for her to shake. "I am Grieve Lewisson, from Myroy Isle. I am to be Lord Ronin's squire."

She eyed his hand suspiciously for a moment, then took it in her own. "Rhona." Her eyes dared him to ask for more than just her name.

All Grieve's instincts screamed that this would be a trap, though what sort, he did not know. "It is a pleasure to meet you, Lady Rhona, guardian of this tree. I have heard tales of naiads, but this is my first time meeting one." He closed his mouth, giving her a challenge of his own.

Her narrowed eyes made him worry that

he'd made a mistake. Perhaps he should have just complimented her on her name the way he had when he'd met Bedelia. Then again, look how well that had turned out.

Then Rhona gave a tiny smile. "I think you mean a dryad, not a naiad. Dryads live in trees. Naiads are river spirits. But both are myths. They don't exist. At least, not outside of stories. And we are both too old for such things."

Grieve recognise the regret in her tone, for he shared it. Life was much simpler as a child, believing all his mother's tales to be true. "Then why protect this tree so passionately?"

"Because it belonged to my mother," she said. "She brought the trees, and many other medicinal plants, when she came to… When she came to live with my father."

"And your father is…?"

She gave him a look of deep disgust. "Not stupid enough to build a fortification out of willows, or anything that burns so easily. Here on Rum Isle, timber is too precious. We build with sod and stone, so our kittens are safe from boys who like to play with fire, and our people sleep safer in their beds, knowing that when Alban raiders come, and they will, they will not be burned alive, for it would take powerful magic indeed to burn down a sod house." A girl she might be, but the hard look at her eyes said she knew as much about war as Grieve himself, or perhaps more. For a moment, she looked like his own father, telling Mahon how to prepare for war. She seized his arm, her touch searing through the cloth as though the flames Grieve had seen earlier were not as imaginary as he thought. "Come. We shall both go to see my father together, and if his witch of a wife is behind this… I will make her rue the day she was born."

Grieve let the girl pulled him into Lord Ronin's house, all the while musing that if one of the two women he'd met today was a witch he would place his wager on Lady Rhona and not the mousey Doireann. But he kept this thought to himself, lest Rhona turn her fury on him again.

Nineteen

"Brigid," Father breathed, his eyes wide.

Rhona glanced down. Had this gown belonged to her mother – her birth mother, not Blanid? That would explain why she'd never seen Blanid wear it. She rubbed her fingers down the silk. She'd treasure it now she knew.

But now she had more important matters to attend to. "Father, why was this boy cutting down trees by the river?"

"Ah, you've met Grieve, your new foster brother," Father said. "He is Lord Lewis' son, and to be treated with every courtesy. As you are not needed here, will you show him around the island and introduce him to everyone? Lord Lewis sent him to help with our defences, so show him everything."

He meant Sanctuary, Rhona knew. Strange that he did not mention its name before Doireann. Did he not trust her either? Rhona could only hope. She moistened her lips. "Yes, Father." She headed upstairs to pack some things to take. A horseback tour of the island could be done in a day, but if she was to show this stranger Sanctuary…she wanted to take her time, to find out if he could be trusted. Unlike Doireann.

Three days, she decided, if they left this afternoon.

She would need riding clothes, not this beautiful gown. The only thing she had left from her mother. Not to mention another cloak, for hers was still covered in mud from when Doireann left her in the woods. Candace had offered to clean it, but Rhona had wanted to show it to her father as proof of his new wife's perfidy. But it could wait until she returned.

As long as Candace took care of the girls.

Rhona headed for her sisters' room, where she could hear giggling.

Candace sat with the three of them, reciting a rhyme that named each of Sive's toes before tickling the small girl.

"Did you tell Father what she did?" Nuala demanded.

Rhona hung her head. "I tried, but he still does not believe me. Mistress Candace, I swear to you that every word I spoke to you and my father is the truth. She has drugged my sisters once, and next time, she might give them more than a simple sleeping potion. She said as much to me before she knocked me out." She rubbed the lump on the back of her head, still tender after almost a week. Who would have thought Doireann could muster so much power in a single blow? "Please, whatever you do, do not let the girls eat or drink anything that Doireann has touched. I trust the staff, for they are all loyal to my father, but they still must obey her. They will tell you if she touches anything in the kitchen, though she hardly goes in there. But if she does – "

"Hush, girl. I will keep them safe. Your mother nursed my girls through a winter fever when I thought I would lose them. Lady Blanid should have sent word when she was taken ill. I would have been here directly to help." Candace smiled.

"But I must go away for a few days. Will you…"

Candace bowed her head. "I will care for the Lady Blanid's girls like they were my own. By the time you return, Lord Ronin will have accepted me into his household as a nurse again. You may not remember your wet nurse, but Lord Ronin remembers me well. I will make sure of it, if he tries to forget."

Did that mean Candace knew who Rhona's real mother was? Rhona opened her mouth to ask.

"Where are you going?" Maeve demanded.

Her sisters could never know. "Father has a new squire, and he wishes me to show him the island. When we return, I will introduce him to you."

"Will he have new stories?" Sive asked, her

eyes shining.

Always, it was stories. If only fairytales were true, and some handsome prince or knight in shining armour would come to save them from Doireann and this war with the Albans.

Rhona managed a smile. "I shall ask him while we ride, and let you know the answer when we return." She made a private wager with herself that the answer would be yes — Grieve had seemed to like telling stories. Perhaps he would have some even she had not heard yet, that he could tell to amuse her on their journey.

Smiling to herself, Rhona headed for her room.

Off came the beautiful golden gown, to be carefully placed in the chest with Blanid's things. She would need a thicker shift — wool instead of linen. She loosened the laces and let the shift slip to the floor.

A male voice swore.

Rhona whirled in panic, and met the eyes of a red-faced Grieve, who turned around as though his life depended on it.

"What are you doing in my chamber?" she

demanded, clutching her shift to her chest.

"I'm not in your chamber, just on the threshold," he said. "Your father told me to follow you, so I did. I waited for you to speak to your sisters, before following you here. How was I to know you intended to undress?"

It sounded reasonable enough. It wasn't like he'd tried to hide.

But…

"Why didn't you say something when I took off my gown? Before I removed my shift?" Rhona demanded. She tugged the woollen shift over her head, so she wouldn't feel so exposed.

"Because I was mesmerised, my lady. It wasn't until I regained my senses that I realised what I should have done. I froze. I could not help myself. I've never seen…" He swallowed, seemingly unable to continue.

"A naked woman before?" she finished for him, feeling her fury build. Oh, if only she could use her magic to blast him out the window. She'd never felt so humiliated in her life.

He managed a watery smile. "Oh, no, I've

seen one of those. A few, actually. Just…never one as beautiful as you. One glimpse and…I lost my mind, my lady. I could no longer think or speak. I could only stare." He ducked his head. "Please accept my forgiveness. I did not mean to offend you. I swear it will not happen again."

Beautiful. He'd called her beautiful. No one ever said that. Well, except her father, and he didn't count. Maybe she would forgive him. After all, she'd never seen a naked man before. She'd probably stare, too.

Instead of the brown overdress she'd intended to wear, Rhona chose the rose-coloured one Blanid had once favoured for festival days, until Maeve was born and her waist thickened too much to tie the laces. Blanid's wine-coloured riding cloak went perfectly with it. Oh, but her hair…

Rhona pulled out the pins and set to work, braiding it in earnest. When she had her hair as firmly under control as the blush that had briefly coloured her cheeks, she turned and said, "Shall we go, Grieve Lewisson?"

Twenty

If he'd known she was about to undress, he would have turned his back on her. That would have been the honourable thing to do. But his breath had caught in his throat as the gown came off, and then her shift…

Yes, he'd seen naked women before. But none of them had such perfect breasts. And nipples as pink as…well, the dress she now wore to hide them. As if anything could hide the swell of her breasts now he'd seen them – they were permanently burned into his brain. He would dream of them for the rest of his days, Grieve was certain of it.

Still he waited for her to slap him like Bedelia had, but she did not.

Then she stood before him, only a breath away, her eyes level with his. Gazing at him expectantly.

"What did you say?" he asked, feeling even more stupid.

She gave him a mischievous smile, as though she'd plucked the thought from his mind and it amused her. "I said, shall we go, Grieve Lewisson?"

He'd never heard his own name sound so…seductive. "Anything you wish, my lady," he managed to say.

"We will not return for a couple of nights, so bring whatever you'll need," she said, bundling a few things together. She tucked the bundle under her arm.

Grieve held out his hand. "Allow me to carry that for you." He might have forgotten his courtesies earlier, but that meant all the more reason to remember them now.

Rhona laughed. "You've seen quite enough of my underthings, Lewisson. You see to your own. I shall meet you in the kitchen."

Feeling his cheeks grow hot all over again – she'd been the one caught naked and unaware, so why was he so much more embarrassed? – he headed for the room he'd been told would be his. A comb, some spare clothes, his cloak…what else did he need? His mind refused to work properly. All he could see was her pale skin, curves he ached to touch…and those breasts!

He gritted his teeth and forced the image out of his head as he descended the stairs two at a time to where his nose told him the kitchen lay.

"I do not know what your father is thinking, Lady Rhona, truly I don't. First her ladyship and now young Lewisson…but you may rest assured that Candace and I will keep an eye on them for you. We are old friends, us two, though the friendship soured a little when she married. We both wanted young Paddy, you see, but he had eyes only for her…"

Grieve stepped inside the room, inhaling the scent of roasting meat and fresh baked bread. He wanted to eat it all.

"He looks like the younger one, not Lewis's heir at all," the woman continued. The cook, Grieve assumed. "Your father and Lewis can't be serious about this."

"Lord Angus himself was a younger son, and now he's Lord of Isla and High Lord of us all. Stranger things have happened in tales as well as in truth. Who can say what will come to pass?" Rhona said. She bit into a crust of bread.

"Who indeed?" Grieve said, reaching for the loaf.

The women's eyes widened – evidently they had not seen him enter.

He tore off a chunk and chewed with relish. No matter what this cook thought of him, at least she would feed him well. "This is the best bread I've tasted in weeks." He swallowed and continued, "I am my father's second surviving son. My brother Mahon will be lord after Father. He will also marry Lord Calum's daughter. Father has not told me about his plans for me, though he sent me here. What do you know that I do not?"

"He expects you to marry one of Father's

daughters and succeed him as Lord of Rum Isle. As I'm the only one old enough, it seems Father has set his sights on giving me to you. Hence this farce about defence and a tour of the island."

Lady Rhona? His? Desire burned deep within him at the thought. If only. But the look in her eyes dispelled that idea as quickly as it had come. Lady Rhona would never accept him as a husband, especially not if her father pushed her to do so.

"Defence against Alban raiders is never a farce. They are a very real threat to us…" Grieve began.

"The boy's right about that. Lewis always was a strategist, and his son must be the same. It can't hurt to have his help defending the place. I will give you as many provisions as the horses can carry, just in case." The cook pulled two loaves from the oven, wrapped them well, then handed them to a maid who carried them outside.

"Come, Lewisson. We may still manage a few miles before dark," Rhona said, leading the way outside.

Two horses stood in the yard, saddled and ready to go. The bread-bearing maid fastened the nearest one's saddlebags. "Safe journey, Lady Rhona," she said with a respectful bow of her head. She glanced at Grieve, but said nothing as she went past.

Bemused, Grieve stared after her. First the cook, now the maids. At home, all would have at least bobbed a curtsey to him, though they'd known him since childhood. Here, things were very different indeed, if the servants had little respect for their betters.

"Wipe that look off your face, Lewisson," Rhona advised him from her perch atop a horse. "Siobhan is betrothed to the first mate on Father's ship. She's not for you."

"No, but you are," he said without thinking. He swung up onto his horse, only to find himself face to face with the furious girl.

"I belong to no man. Not my father, not you, and definitely no one who even thinks a woman can be owned. No self-respecting Islander woman would allow such a thing. I choose to take you on a tour of Rum Isle because my knowledge of the island is second only to my father's, and you might be able to help us defend our home against all enemies."

Now it was Grieve's turn to bow his head. "I am your servant, as I am your father's squire, Lady Rhona. I am indebted to you for your kindness, I'm sure. All enemies of such a lovely lady are, of course, my enemies as well."

She almost smiled at that, but when he looked again, the smile was gone as though he'd imagined it. "Pretty words, Lewisson. You'll need more than words if it comes to war." She set off at a fast trot, and it took Grieve a moment before he could persuade his horse to follow, by which time she was several lengths ahead of him.

He feared she always would be, but that didn't stop him from striving to catch up. Lady Rhona was a woman he wanted to catch, but only if she allowed it.

Twenty-One

Rhona headed for the eastern watchtower, reasoning that it was the only suitable place to take him that was an easy ride before dark. Sanctuary could be reached just as easily, for they didn't have a cart, but she wasn't sure she was ready to show that to him yet. Better to take him on a full tour of the island and see what kind of man he truly was before revealing any secrets. Lord Lewis was no fool – if he'd sent his son to help Father, then Grieve could help. But if he was a strategist like his father…he might use Rum Isle as a pawn in a much larger game with higher stakes than Rhona could see. Rum Isle might not be important to Lord Lewis and his son, but it was everything to those who lived there.

"Are you planning on pitching me off a cliff, my lady?" Grieve asked after some time.

Rhona smiled. To someone who didn't know what to look for, the clifftop watchtowers looked like ordinary crags. "Maybe later. You have not yet vexed me enough for that. Perhaps on the third offence I will not be as forgiving."

She dismounted, and glanced over her shoulder to see what Grieve had made of her half-joking response.

"I shall endeavour not to cut down any trees, or look at you, without your permission. Is there anything else you'd care to warn me about, so I do not offend you again?" He lifted his hand. "Wait, I already know I must be kind to kittens."

"It is always wise to be kind to kittens," Rhona said. She headed for the standing stone that marked the entrance, then slipped into the rock crevice behind it. It was a tight squeeze, but grown men used this passage every day, so she knew she would fit. When she was through, she extended a hand. "Come, Lewisson, if you wish to see Rum Isle's first line of defence against invaders."

He grumbled as he squeezed through the gap, then stood beside her. "A cave." He did not sound impressed.

Rhona laughed. "Rum Isle is full of caves, some on the land, and some on the cliffs, and some you can only reach at high or low tide, for the ocean hides a veritable army of rocks to keep Rum Isle safe. The ancient peoples of the isles found this one, and improved upon it." She led him deeper into the shadows to the steps. Twisted and winding, worn by the tread of generations of boots, the steps led up into the tower, or at least that's what they called the top of the crag. The roof of the top cavern had caved in, leaving it open to the elements, but with a clear view all the way to Alba on a clear day. Today, like most days, it was hidden in mist, but she could still see for miles. As could tonight's watchman.

"Good evening, Lady Rhona," he said.

"Good evening indeed, Ximeno," she said. "This is Grieve Lewisson, my father's new squire from Myroy Isle. My father wants him to see all our defences. Where is Nuno?"

"He said he would go get our dinner from Mother. Did you not see him?" When Rhona shook her head, Ximeno continued, "Then he must have met a pretty girl, who distracted him."

Grieve burst out laughing, then stopped when he realised he was the only one.

"What's funny?" Rhona asked coolly.

Grieve was still grinning. "Why, doesn't he mean you? But we saw no one on the way here…"

"Nuno is sweet on Ciara, though I am not sure if she is as sweet on him. He makes frequent visits to his mother, though, hoping to see her, so Belen encourages him, even if Ciara gives him no hope." Rhona sniffed. If she wanted a man, she would not toy with his affections like Ciara. Though it seemed to drive Nuno wild, so perhaps she knew her man better than Rhona thought. Still… "Ximeno, can you tell him how we run things here? I'll unsaddle the horses for the night."

Without another word, she hurried down the steps and away from the only man on Rum Isle who thought she was worth looking at.

Twenty-Two

Grieve watched her go, too bewildered to ask why. Ximeno just shrugged, then began to point out the features of their clifftop eyrie, including what Grieve had taken for an eagle's nest but was actually a watchfire which could be seen from the other three towers when it was lit. He stroked the smooth stone, shaped into a natural tower with only a little help from men. The other towers Ximeno pointed out looked almost identical to this one – natural formations that no one would look twice at, approaching the island for the first time.

Unlike the wooden watchtowers at Isla and Myroy, which stood out for what they were.

When Ximeno's spiel seemed to wind down, the man took Grieve's arm and looked around before dropping to a whisper. "A word of advice, if I may. Lady Rhona might not be the prettiest girl on the island, but it is cruel to mock her for it. She is the best healer on Rum Isle, perhaps in all of the Southern Isles, and it does not matter if a man must look upon her face instead of his sweetheart's when the lady's help is needed. And she's still the Lady of the Isle — when she marries, her husband will be Lord Ronin's successor, for his claim will go to her. If you intend to stay here, it is not wise to offend Lady Rhona."

"She's already talked about throwing me off a cliff," Grieve admitted, but his thoughts were more on Ximeno's words than his own. Not the prettiest girl on the island? Had Ximeno even looked at the girl? Even clothed, she was lovely. Tall and fair as a Viken, perhaps taller than any other woman he'd seen on Rum Isle, but far from ugly.

"Then you had best guard your tongue most

carefully. You must have offered Lady Rhona a grievous insult to offend her so," Ximeno said. "She will be a true lady when her father passes, much like her mother was. Nothing like the new one. They say she throws screeching tantrums if her whims are not acted upon, and never does a thing for anyone. Why, we found her with a cart bogged in the mud the other day, partway home. She beat Nuno with a stick when he didn't get the cart wheel free fast enough. If you ask me, Lord Ronin should get that one pregnant as quickly as possible, and hope the childbed fever takes her like it did his first wife. Poor Lady Blanid. Lady Rhona must be heartbroken even her healing arts could not save her."

"I…thank you," Grieve said. "I should probably help Lady Rhona with…the horses." He stumbled down the uneven steps, wondering how the watchman managed not to break his neck each time he had to race down them to report a raiding party.

"So, do you still think we're defenceless?" Rhona greeted him.

"There's a saying on Myroy that as long as a

man still has his wits, he will never be defenceless," Grieve said, stretching his frozen fingers out toward the fire. "I never said Rum Isle was without defences, just that it would benefit from stronger ones." He drew in a deep breath, hoping to inhale courage with the air. Something to stop his knees from shaking, as he added, "And when your watchman spoke of a pretty girl, of course I thought he meant it as a compliment to you. Why would he not? Why, just look at you."

"I believe you already did that, this afternoon," Rhona said dryly.

As if on command, Grieve's cheeks reddened. "I said I was sorry for staring, but I'll never be sorry for seeing what I saw. A vision of loveliness no man would want to forget. And I'll challenge any man who dares say otherwise."

She shook her head, but there was a smile on her lips. "Pretty words, Lewisson, no more. I am not so vain as to wish I were the most beautiful girl in the Southern Isles – I know my own reflection, and I am content. I'm sure your flattery is well meant, though unnecessary. I've already set out our bedrolls, and you may share my bed tonight." She gestured at a stone alcove, where Grieve saw his things beside hers.

His mouth dropped open, but he couldn't think of a word to say. He stared, yet he could detect no hint of laughter in her expression. She expected him to share her bed?

"I…I thought it was customary to start with a kiss," he said.

Uncertainty flared in her eyes. For all her forwardness, she was as nervous as he was.

Grieve grew bolder, stepping forward so that he could embrace her. He lifted a tentative hand to her cheek, which was as soft as he'd imagined it to be. "So beautiful," he murmured.

Her lips parted, but no sound came out.

Gently, oh so carefully, he touched his lips to hers. Her slight gasp dared him to do more, as her fingers tangled in his hair, holding him close. Only then did he dare to tease her tongue with his, and the taste of her, the softness of the woman in his arms, was enough for him to lose his mind. Once he'd started, he could not stop kissing her – no, not even to draw a breath that had not caressed her breast first with its airy fingers.

By the time Rhona pushed him away, her eyes blazed with the same desire coursing through his veins. With trembling hands, he unfastened his cloak and dropped it on the stone floor. Then he seized the hem of his tunic…

Her hand covered his, pulling the hem down. "Keep your clothes on, Myroy boy. I said you may lie with me – to keep warm, for 'tis cold in this cave, even with the fire going. If I want you to be my lover, I'll tell you so, but not tonight. Though that was a fine kiss. If I do choose you for a lover, I'd hope for many more such kisses."

He stepped away and straightened his tunic. "My apologies, my lady. Your beauty bewitched me again. If you desire another kiss, you have only to ask."

She laid a hand on his chest. "Rhona. You are a lord's son, and I am a lord's daughter. After sharing a kiss like that…we should at least be friends."

"Only if you call me Grieve, the name my mother gave me. And accept that when I say you are beautiful, I mean every word. If other men cannot see it, then they are fools."

She took a deep breath, looking as enervated by the exchange as he felt. "Very well, though it is strange to think every man I have ever known is a fool. Doesn't it seem more likely that the one man who sees things differently is more foolish than the rest? Grieve?"

It was strange yet lovely to her his name on her lips once more. He wanted to hear her gasp it, moan it, maybe even scream it for joy. One day, he promised himself.

"If I am a fool, then I do not know it. How would I know? Ah, I have heard some kings keep fools in their courts, who amuse them by telling tales. Shall I share some of the stories I know, and see if they amuse you?"

Rhona sat beside the fire and broke a loaf in two, before handing him half. "Tell all the tales you want. If you tell me one I have not heard, then I will open a bottle of my father's best wine. Belen slipped one into the saddlebags."

A challenge, the likes of which no Myroy man could refuse. Grieve took the bread and began, "Once upon a time…"

Twenty-Three

Shuffling footsteps woke Grieve. A man tiptoed through the cave, taking exaggerated care to make as little noise as possible as he ascended the steps. Nuno, he assumed, for the man looked like last night's watchman, his brother.

Grieve took a deep breath, and inhaled an unfamiliar floral scent. He glanced down. He'd shared Rhona's bed, just as she'd promised, but he had not expected to share tales with her half the night until he'd fallen asleep with her warm weight in his arms. Now, the fully clothed girl was pressed against his side, one arm flung across his belly as if to claim him. Her hand was dangerously close to where he dreamed she'd caressed him. Where he wished she'd touch him now, for he stood to attention for her in anticipation of a more intimate embrace than the one they were in now.

If his father and Lord Ronin sought to matchmake him with Rhona, then he would embrace their plan with all his strength.

"Marry me, Rhona," he whispered into her hair.

He snorted softly. He'd known the woman for a day, but he knew he'd never get her out of his head.

Rhona shifted, and her hand drifted lower, then fastened around him. By all that was holy, how could he feel the heat of her touch through his tunic? Whatever she touched, she burned.

"Well, you're a big one, aren't you? Dreaming about some girl back home?" she asked, giving him an agonisingly good squeeze before letting go.

Grieve swallowed. "Thinking about the girl

in my arms right now," he said. "The beautiful Lady Rhona."

She shifted away from him and sat up. "No good morning kisses for you, then. You go take care of that, for we have a long ride ahead of us. I must show you the rest of the island, and tonight, we'll sleep in Sanctuary. The island's biggest secret of all."

Already his arms felt empty without her, but Grieve did as she said. Riding with a raging hard-on for the woman beside him would make for a hell of a day.

Twenty-Four

Perhaps it had been the wine, or all those well-told tales, but as she'd cuddled up to Grieve's warm body in her bedroll that night, Rhona knew she'd made her decision. She would show him Sanctuary. But not because her father had ordered it. No, she'd show him because she wanted him to stay and become one of them.

She'd known him for a day, and yet it felt like she'd known him forever. An easy familiarity had sprung between them last night, like they were a long-lost brother and sister.

Yet that kiss…no, that had not been brotherly at all. While her lips were locked with his, she'd seriously considered taking things further, perhaps even letting him make love to her. She'd never thought much about marriage, but she did know one thing – she'd not go to her marriage bed as some virgin maiden who'd never known a man's touch. No, when she took a husband, she'd already know he was a skilled lover.

If Grieve could set her body aflame with a single kiss, imagine what he could do with the rest of his body…and hers…

She dreamed he'd asked her to marry him, but before she could answer, she awoke. Perhaps that was for the best, for she'd found him pitching a tent in his tunic with a look of panic on his face lest she notice. She'd have to be blind indeed not to notice he carried a mighty sword beneath his belt as well as the one that hung from it.

Idly, she wondered what it would feel like to have that length of hot, hard flesh slide inside her, as his hands caressed her and he told her over and over again how beautiful she was.

Rhona almost laughed aloud. A daydream, that's what it was, conjured out of the silly stories they'd told last night. Knights and princess, genies and sultans, courtesans and princesses…all living happily ever after, with no thoughts of war or what might happen in the future. If only life were like the stories.

If it were, then she and Grieve could lie abed, making love to each other so that every moment was happy ever after. But not today, for Nuno had returned, and that meant Ximeno would want their cave to sleep in after standing watch all night. So she freshened up and broke her fast, while Grieve readied himself for the ride along the western side of the island, before they headed to Sanctuary.

The prettier side of the island, some said, because it was the side furthest from Alba. But it was also the least sheltered part of the island, for there was nothing to stop the waves from rolling in and smashing against the cliffs. The spray flew so high Rhona tasted salt on her lips more than once.

If she were to kiss Grieve again, would his lips be salty, too? Her eyes met his and a smile lifted her lips almost of its own volition. Her heart raced as though she'd galloped along the clifftop, instead of keeping to the slow pace such uneven terrain demanded. Grieve was several yards away, yet he'd stolen her breath somehow.

Perhaps…

"What do you think of the plot between my father and yours?" she asked him.

"Which one?"

"The one to make us marry."

Grieve reined his horse to a stop, and Rhona's mount almost collided with his. Close enough to touch, and he did, capturing her hand in his own. "I know nothing of any plot, for the gossip in your kitchen was the first I had heard of it. But the more I think on it, every moment I spend with you, the less I care whether there is a plot at all." He pressed his lips to her hand, a chaste kiss compared to the one they'd shared last night. "I would like to kiss you again, Lady Rhona, and with you in my thoughts, there is no space for anyone else." For a moment, his eyes were dark and full of feeling, before he turned away to gaze toward the horizon. "But you must show me all of Rum Isle's defences. I must make sure…the island…is protected."

The love that had blossomed in her breast as she anticipated another delightful kiss shrivelled in the summer sun as Grieve put more distance between them.

Rhona sighed. She dreamed too much, she knew, for there were too many stories in her head. Grieve was right to be practical about these things, for love could not stop a war.

Twenty-Five

Grieve cursed his clumsiness with words, and with women. For a moment there, it seemed they'd shared the same thoughts, and then it had all gone wrong. Was he supposed to say he heartily approved of their fathers' plot? That couldn't be right – she had made it very clear that she would follow her own heart, not her father's plans.

He scarcely paid attention as she showed him the other three watchtowers and the harbour, introducing him to everyone they met. He smiled and nodded and shook hands, accepting more cups of ale than was good for him.

More than once, he'd had to take a trip into the bushes, to Rhona's amusement.

On the third such detour, she'd waited until he'd climbed back onto his horse before she said, "At least you gave me a show of your own this time. 'Tis a fine arse you have, Lewisson. A mite pale, but I don't suppose it sees much sun."

She'd been watching him piss? Grieve's face grew so hot he feared his skin would crisp off. And then…he smiled, at the knowledge that she'd been watching him. Maybe she was not as cold to him as he'd thought.

He hurried to catch up to her. "Are there any other parts of me you consider fine?" he called.

She tossed her head. "I'm sure I'd have to see more of such parts before I could make a judgement like that."

He drew even with her. "And what parts of me would you like to see more of, my lady?"

She darted a glance at him, then looked away. "I'm sure I don't know. But you have seen all of me, so it seems only fitting that I should see all of you. And I thought we agreed to use first names, not…anything else."

"So we did. And if my lady wishes to see all of me, she has only to ask."

She closed her eyes. "Grieve…"

"Yes, Rhona?"

"Stop. We have arrived."

Grieve looked around. "This is no sanctuary. A sheltered depression, out of the wind, with the river running alongside, but it is too open. The enemy would only need to follow your trail here, and there would be no escape. You'd be slaughtered."

"And yet no enemy has ever taken Rum Isle," Rhona said softly. "You see that waterfall?"

Grieve's gazed followed her pointing finger. "It's pretty," he said cautiously.

Rhona laughed. She slid down and began to unfasten her saddle. She gave her horse a slap on the rump in dismissal and carried her things toward the waterfall.

Grieve hurried to do the same. But the buckles refused to unfasten, so by the time he'd freed his horse, Rhona was nowhere to be seen.

"Rhona?" he called, feeling like a fool. He set off for the waterfall, wondering if he would see her from there.

The waterfall turned pink, before she emerged from behind it, brushing water droplets from her cloak. "Are you coming, or are you waiting for an enemy army to appear?"

It was another natural watchtower, Grieve guessed, as he scrambled up the damp rocks to where Rhona stood.

"Come and see," she said, turning to lead the way.

He was surprised to find the entrance was big enough to walk through without ducking his head or turning sideways – unlike the watchtowers she'd shown him. The passage beyond narrowed as it led upward, and he left his saddle beside hers, shouldering his bags so they wouldn't catch on the walls. The combination of slippery stone and the sharp incline made it a challenge to keep his footing, but Grieve managed to follow Rhona without actually falling, though he slipped twice. He noticed several passages that led to the left and right, but Rhona did not turn, and he had no choice but to follow where she led.

Then she stopped so suddenly that he slammed into her, wrapping his arms around her to keep from knocking her over.

"Welcome to Sanctuary," she said, glancing over her shoulder at him. "And if that's your saddlebags I can feel digging into my shoulder, I think you've just squashed the bread."

Grieve realised he still held her, and reluctantly relinquished the woman he only wanted to pull closer. He mumbled an apology.

"This is Rum Island's stronghold. None have ever taken it, and none shall while Islanders hold it," Rhona said.

Grieve could see why. The place was like one of the legendary ancient fortresses – in fact, it probably was one. The cavern was huge – his father's great hall would fit in here twice over, with space to spare. Why, you could fit most of Myroy Island's people in here. A stream ran along one side of the cavern, presumably an offshoot of the river that fed the waterfall at the door.

In the light of the flames of the firepit, which was already lit, though Rhona could not have been here long enough to light such a fire, Grieve could just discern steps at the opposite end of the cavern, spiralling upwards.

"Is there a watchtower atop here, too?" he asked.

She nodded. "Two, actually, though they are not so much towers as higher caverns through which the river used to flow. The island is riddled with caves, but these are the highest and the biggest. From the east spire, you can see clear to the sea, and with men in both east and west, two men can keep watch over the whole island, while our people live comfortably in the cavern below. There are smaller caverns, branching off. Some are store rooms, while others belong to particular families who have lived on Rum Isle for generations. There used to be a cavern where we kept our horses, but the roof collapsed and no one has yet shifted the rubble. The main cavern is a meeting place, an underground village square, where the cook fire is kept burning while anyone resides here."

"Ah, so that's why the fire is lit! Here I thought you must have some magical means of making a blaze so quickly, but the watchmen here must keep the fire burning instead." Grieve grinned at his own joke.

Rhona didn't seem to find it funny. Instead, she seemed lost for words.

"Are you going to introduce me to the watchmen of Sanctuary? Which spire first, east or west?" he prompted.

"There is no one here but us. The watchmen of the cliff towers retreat to Sanctuary when their families are here, but in summer it is empty but for the harvest, stored for when we need it in winter." She blinked, then seemed to regain a little of her earlier enthusiasm. "Would you like to see my family's cavern? It's called the Lady's Chamber, because it's usually the Lady of Rum Isle who leads her people here, while the lord and his men defend the island long enough for their families to reach safety."

She led the way along the stream, then crossed a set of stepping stones to the far bank. Behind a rock pillar was a third set of steps Grieve hadn't seen before, and light glimmered at the top.

"Do the men of the isles make it to Sanctuary, or is it a fight to the death?" Grieve asked. Not that any Islander would run from a fight – they were not cowards. But Alba had many more men than the Islanders could muster, and anything Grieve could do to make sure the Islanders lived to fight another day, he must.

"Sometimes," Rhona said. "The cliffs are a natural defence, and every man on Rum Isle must keep a bow with a number of arrows. They are supposed to practice archery every day, too, but I fear they have been lax of late. It has been a long time since Albans last raided our shores. Most of the heroic tales of this place are about the courage of ladies, not men, though. And some include commanding the army of archers, when our men are away."

She reached the top of the steps, and edged to the side so that Grieve might enter the cavern beside her.

Light streaked down from a hole in the

roof, sparkling through the waterfall that splashed down into a pool which overflowed into a second cascade that undoubtedly fed the stream below.

Grieve laughed. "Are you sure it's not called the Lady's Chamber because it has a bath in it?"

Rhona smiled. "It's not a bath I'd enter by choice. The water is icy cold, so it's better to take a bucket of it and set it by the fire to warm before you wash." She cupped some in her hands and drank. "Freezing, but as pure as anything you'll find on Rum Isle. Taste it yourself."

Grieve knelt beside the pool and cupped his hands.

Rhona made a sound between a squeak and a scream.

Grieve jumped to his feet, his hand flying to the hilt of his sword.

But there was no enemy to fight, or at least none that would take damage from a sword.

Rhona stood in the middle of a puddle of water that must have come from the roof, which had soaked her to the skin on its way down. "Can you get me some dry clothes, please?" she asked.

"Of course." Grieve hurried down to the main cavern, grabbed her saddle bags and raced back up the steps.

When he reached the chamber, the bags dropped from his hands and he lost the ability to speak.

Twenty-Six

The moment Grieve left, Rhona stripped off her wet clothes and used the dry parts to mop the water from her skin. After the long day's ride, she needed a wash, though this wasn't how she'd imagined it.

What was taking Grieve so long? Could he not find her bags? Rhona scanned the cavern, looking for the chests her family kept here. The clothes and blankets would certainly be in need of an airing, but a musty tunic was better than nothing.

Ah, there they were — stacked by the

sleeping alcoves. She pried open the catch on the topmost one and lifted out blanket after blanket, looking for the clothing she knew had to be here somewhere. It wasn't until she reached the bottom of the chest that she encountered what felt like a sleeping fur, but when she pulled it out, it turned out to be a winter cloak made of sealskin. She rubbed the velvety fur against her cheek, remembering when this cloak had belonged to her grandmother and she used to bury her face in it.

Something fell to the floor behind her.

Rhona swung the cloak around her shoulders, holding it closed with one hand as she whirled to face the intruder.

"By all that's holy…" She marched up to Grieve. "You're making a habit of catching me with my clothes off. A vainer lady than I might think you like what you see so much, you wish to see it again."

"I do." The words had no sooner left his lips than he turned as pale as mist. "I mean — "

Rhona held her cloak open. "There, then. Look your fill, and may your eyes burn out of

your head after the devil is done with you, for
_ "

"My God, you're beautiful."

Now Rhona was the one lost for words. Grieve stepped forward and kissed her, drawing her body against his warmth, and cocooning the rest of her in the cloak. This man could kiss her forever, if he wished, but Rhona became increasingly aware of something hard pressed against her hip. She glanced down, and forced herself to break that irresistible kiss.

"Stop poking me with your sword," she said.

Grieve turned red as he glanced down, too. "I'm sorry, my lady, but like I said, you're beautiful…"

"No, not that sword. Take it off!" Before she could think the idea through, she unbuckled his belt and let it drop to the floor, sword and all. "Better. Now, kiss me again."

"I think it would be best if I obeyed your earlier order, my lady. The one where you asked me to get your clothes. Because if I kiss you again, while you are like this…" Grieve gestured at her body, the longing clear in his eyes as he looked at her. "I fear I will forget all thoughts of chivalry and honour, as though the devil himself sat on my shoulder, whispering in my ear. I will already pay a painful penance for the thoughts in my head right now."

But Rhona's blood was afire, and so was his. She was certain of it. "It is me you owe penance to, staring at my body so. It seems only right that I should get to do the same." She reached for the hem of his tunic, and tugged it up over his head.

"Lady Rhona, I think if I were naked, too, it would only make things all the harder."

Her breathing came fast now. "Then you should take off your hose, so we can do something about that."

Despite his half-hearted protests, Grieve soon stood naked before her, wearing nothing but his cloak. Now it was Rhona's turn to look her fill, at the lean, muscled man before her. Yes, oh yes. He was everything she could want in a man. In a lover.

She threw herself at him, twining her arms around his neck as she kissed him deeply. As her breasts met his hard chest, her body seemed to flame to life, just as she knew it should. She reached around to cup his butt cheeks, which were every bit as firm as they'd looked. But that only pressed other parts of him harder, more insistently into her belly, demanding more.

More that she wanted to give.

Rhona drew him down to the pile of blankets, letting out a contented sigh as his weight settled atop her. Then his lips descended to her breasts, kissing, sucking, setting off currents deep inside.

"Yes, oh yes…" She scarcely recognised her own voice, so breathless with need.

She wrapped her legs around his hips, wanting to feel him everywhere. She reached down to stroke him, guiding him to where she wanted him.

She cried out as she felt something hot slide inside of her, but it was too small to be what she wanted. His fingers, she realised. "I want you, Grieve. All of you."

"I'm your first. I can feel it. I don't want to hurt you."

Yet his fingers stroked her, driving her mad

with desire for what she really wanted. Taunting, tempting, tantalising…tipping her over a cliff she'd never seen, into bliss. For the first time in her life, she soared in a man's hands. This was better than her dreams.

"Grieve, I need you. Please." It came out as a joyful sob in a voice Rhona still didn't recognise as her own.

His eyes darkened with desire as he lifted his head to meet her eyes. "Rhona, are you sure?"

She'd never been so sure of anything in her life. "Make love to me, Grieve."

He grasped her hips, the hard heat of him replacing where his fingers had stroked her only moments before. He thrust what felt like a burning brand inside her, searing her insides until he filled her completely. And it felt so good.

Breathlessly, she urged him on, moaning as the molten heat that was him moved inside her. Again and again and again. Until she could no longer control the bliss she felt, and screamed his name.

Dimly, she heard her own name on his lips, before he leaned forward to kiss her.

She looked up, lost in his eyes, as she clenched around the part of him still inside her. This was what she wanted. "Marry me, Grieve," she said.

He stared at her, then began to laugh. As he sat up, he withdrew from her, leaving her emptier than she'd ever felt before. He headed for the pool to clean himself up. Only when he was done splashing, did he stop laughing.

Rhona wrapped herself in her cloak, wanting to relive the memory of his touch, branding it into her skin for every moment they were apart. "What's funny?" she asked.

"I thought a lady expected a marriage proposal before she shared her bed, not after," he said.

Rhona shrugged. "I can't imagine why any woman would agree to marry a man before knowing what sort of lover he was. When I agree to share my bed with one man for the rest of my life, it will not be a stranger who I have not touched."

He brought a dripping cloth to where she lay, and held it out. "I fear I am a messy lover. I scarcely know what possessed me, just that I wanted to possess you. I hope I did not hurt you. There is a little blood..." He pressed the cloth to her thigh, and steam rose up into the air. The cold water was chilly against her burning skin, but Rhona relished it, even more as Grieve stroked her thighs with the wet cloth in an intimate caress that promised she would know no better lover than him.

She covered his hand with hers. "You didn't hurt me. That was...wonderful. I want you to share my bed again tonight."

He swallowed. "For warmth, like last night? For I give you fair warning, my lady. I will do my best to honour you as you deserve while I am awake, but I fear my dreams. After knowing the joy of your beautiful body, I know my dreams will be filled with you. And if my hands stray onto your body as I sleep, it is because I long to make love to you all over again."

Again? Twice in one night? Never had she heard of a man visiting his wife's bed more than once in a night. The thought was thrilling...tantalising...too much for her to resist.

"Then I insist we sleep naked. I long to feel you inside me again."

"As my lady commands."

Twenty-Seven

Three times he'd made love to her, each time more delightful than the last. If he'd had the stamina, Grieve would have loved her all night, until the dawn light kissed her cheeks, for he'd never met a girl so eager, or so angelic when she cried out his name for the joy he'd brought her.

But would it be enough? Doubt gnawed at him, after what she'd said last night. That she wouldn't marry a man unless he was the sort of lover she wanted in her bed for the rest of her life.

He slipped out of the bed they'd made of the blankets on the floor, and headed for the pool to wash himself once more. He dressed, then headed to the cavern to see to breakfast. Perhaps he could bring it to her, so that she might break her fast in bed.

He found the bread he'd squashed last night, along with some hard cheese. If she still slept, then he could offer her a hot breakfast. Grieve set about coaxing the fire into life from the embers. When he had a decent blaze going, he set about melting the cheese and toasting the bread.

"Grieve?"

He'd taken so long, Rhona was not only awake, but dressed for the day, her fingers working to braid her hair so quickly it seemed to require no thought on her part at all.

"I'm making breakfast." He waved at the toast, which had started to burn. Hastily, he pulled the bread out of the fire and blew the flames out. "I was going to bring it to you."

"It was cold without you." Her eyes said so much more.

Grieve's mouth grew drier than the toast in

his hands. He set the cheese on it and held it out. "Careful, it's hot."

She took the offering with both hands, smiling. "I like things hot." She lifted her lips for a kiss.

Grieve wiped the worst of the crumbs off his hands, then carefully cupped her face. So beautiful, and that fire in her eyes… He touched his lips to hers, and for that moment, they shared the passion of their night together. He wanted to unlace her gown and do it all over again, but he wasn't sure how long it would take to return to her father's house. Where Grieve fully intended to ask Lord Ronin for her hand, and every other bit connected to it, too.

"You must be a witch, for you have cast a spell over me," he said.

Rhona stiffened in his arms. "I have done no such thing." She pulled away, putting several yards between them before sitting down to break her fast.

Curse his clumsy tongue. Grieve concentrated on making his own breakfast, while he tried to work out what to say to make things right.

Finally, he settled for: "Lady Rhona, if anything I have done has offended you, then I am deeply sorry. I only meant that I am so in love I cannot think straight any more, for all my thoughts are of you. If you are willing..." He turned, hoping to meet her eyes before he dropped to his knees, as custom demanded.

But Rhona was gone. She hadn't heard a word.

Grieve swore, then bit into his bread and cheese, burned his tongue, and swore some more.

He fell silent when the scrape of booted feet at the entrance alerted him that he was not alone any more.

"Rhona?" he asked tentatively, hoping she had returned.

Instead, a child emerged from the passage, followed by another, then an older woman holding the hand of a third. "Good thing you have the fire going, young man, for we'll need it. The Albans picked a cold, clear day to attack, thinking we'd be huddled around our fires and not watching for them. More fool them, I say."

"Albans? Where?" Rhona appeared on the stepping stones, concern wrinkling her forehead. "Candace, where is my father?"

The woman looked grim. "He set off yesterday for Isla. Something about a declaration of war from Alba. This is the start of it, I'm sure."

Rhona nodded, watching more people enter the cave – some of them the women Grieve had met in her father's kitchens. The whole household was here.

"Where is Lady Doireann?" Candace asked.

The cook shook her head. "She threw a mighty fit, saying she would not leave a scrap for the Albans to steal. We left her trying to put more things in a cart than it could carry. When one of the men told her so, she ordered him away, saying she would drive the cart here herself."

Rhona swore, using words Grieve had rarely heard from a lady. "Then she's even more of a fool than I thought, for she does not even know the way. I'll go fetch her."

The cook seized her arm. "Lady Rhona,

don't. If the Albans capture you, your father will never forgive us."

"He will also not forgive us if we leave Doireann to die, or worse," Rhona said grimly. "Stay here. I shall go alone."

Grieve jumped to his feet. "No you shall not! I should be the one to go."

Rhona glared at him, then subsided. "Fine. You may come with me." She trotted up the steps and returned with her cloak around her shoulders, and a bundle of cloth that she shoved into Grieve's arms. "Put this on. You'll need it."

The sweet girl who'd shared his bed was gone. In her place stood a cold-hearted warrior, like the Vikens she resembled. Grieve had never been frightened of a woman before, but right now, Rhona was terrifying.

He buckled on his sword belt, but decided to wait until they got outside to don his cloak. He wished he'd brought armour with him, but what he had was back at Lord Ronin's house, along with his other weapons. The sooner they got there, the better.

Twenty-Eight

Rhona only glanced behind her once to make sure Grieve was following her before she set off at a gallop for home. She'd be there by noon – she only hoped it would be soon enough to get Doireann to safety. Doireann had lost everything to raiders once – it would be needlessly cruel to allow it to happen again. Rhona might not like the woman, but she couldn't bring herself to hate her that much.

Her thoughts were occupied with a far more important question: was she willing to reveal her magic to save Doireann, if that's what it took? For to do so would be to reveal that she wasn't Father's legitimate daughter, but the result of a union between him and a witch. As her father's bastard, she had no claim over Rum Isle, and neither Grieve or his father would want such a union. If she had to use magic to save Doireann, then she would lose Grieve.

But if she let the Albans harm Doireann, then her father would probably disown her, no matter who her husband was. And she couldn't live with herself, knowing she'd sacrificed another woman for her own happiness.

But if her father found out she was a bastard, he'd probably disown her anyway, so no matter what she did, Rhona would lose her home here.

Tears blurred her vision, but Rhona wiped them away. This was not a time for self-pity. She had to do what was right, and damn the consequences. She might not like Doireann, but the woman was still family, albeit by marriage, and no one hurt her family. Least of all a bunch of Alban scum.

She wove through the woods, trusting

Grieve to keep up, as they neared her home. As they reached the last of the trees, Rhona dismounted, and tied her horse where it would be out of view of the house. She gestured for Grieve to do the same.

"We'll be too high if we climb the ridge on horseback. On foot, we can creep up on the house unseen. If the raiders have already arrived and we are too late...I do not want to give them any warning of our arrival," she said.

"My weapons are in the house. If I can get them, I will be more use to you than I am now with just a sword," Grieve whispered.

Rhona nodded, not wanting to voice her thoughts. If the Albans had not yet arrived, Grieve would have no need of his weapons, and all that would matter was the speed with which they got Doireann away. If the Albans had arrived before them...then Grieve's weapons were as good as lost, and nothing would save Doireann but a powerful show of magic. And that would cost her everything she held dear.

They crept up the slope, keeping low until they reached the shelter of the stones at the top. As a child, she'd traced the carvings on them and wondered what they meant, but now all her attention was on the beach at the base of the cliffs.

Her heart sank. The Alban boats had already beached themselves on the sand, and aside from a pair of boys they'd left on guard, the men were nowhere to be seen.

They might have gone inland, attacking farms and crofts. But the biggest house closest to the beach was her father's, on the cliffs overlooking the beach. They'd be fools not to go there first.

"They might already be at the house," she told Grieve. "Best we use the cover by the river to get closer."

He nodded, and followed her down the hill to the river. Grieve was quieter on his feet than she thought he'd be – she had to glance behind her more than once to make sure he was still there, but he was, as intent as she was on making this rescue work.

If only they weren't too late.

If Doireann was dead…

Then none of the Albans would leave here

alive, Rhona swore.

They'd raped Aunt Blanid, sentenced her mother Brigid to a lifetime taking care of her sister with no chance of marriage, and destroyed Doireann's home and family. She'd be damned before she allowed them to take any more from her family.

Grieve reached the willow trees first, crouching behind a trunk that still bore the marks from his axe. "We're too late," he whispered.

No. They couldn't be. Rhona dropped to her knees and peered through the forked trunk of what had been the first willow on Rum Isle.

In the yard that had always been the heart of her father's household stood perhaps a dozen Albans, clearly recognisable in their piss-yellow tunics. They'd be pissing themselves in fear by the time she was done with them. Rhona rose, careful to keep hidden behind the seaward tree trunk. She bit her lip until she tasted blood, taking her time choosing her target.

"Bring her to me!"

The shouted command had their attention, and Rhona's, too.

Doireann appeared, marched between two men who each had a hold of one of her arms.

Rhona changed her mind about the spell, swapping fire for air, as she sent a breeze through the yard that carried Doireann's words to her.

"Please don't hurt me. I did as I was bid!" she insisted. "All the riches of Rum Isle. I know where they are!"

Maybe a fire spell was called for, after all. A fire spell that turned that treacherous bitch into a ball of flame.

"Where?" A man with fancy armour over his yellow tunic stepped up to her.

"A cave in the woods. They're all there. I can show you…if you promise to let me go." Doireann fell to her knees. "Please, sir. You spared me on Scitis so that I could come here to find out what you wish to know."

The man laughed. "You would betray your new husband so easily?"

Doireann spat on the ground. "Lord Ronin is no husband to me, if he's even a man at all. He would not share my bed, not even on our wedding night. There's no marriage between us, and no love either. He forces me to run after his unruly brats like a servant, but won't give me a child of my own. You can have his island, and all that's on it. All I ask is that you let me go so that I might find a real man to be my husband."

"After you have shown us this cave, woman. Then we shall see."

"Let me…let me get the cart, so it will be easier to bring everything back." Doireann clambered to her feet, then took a tentative step toward the pony cart.

Rhona bit her lip, readying a fireball. The moment Doireann climbed atop that cart, Rhona would set it ablaze.

"Ooh, look, a Viken spy," a voice said behind Rhona. Then something crashed into the back of her head and darkness descended.

Twenty-Nine

Grieve had only a moment to reach for his sword, but he was too slow. One blow felled Rhona, and the second sent him half-stunned to the ground. He tried to fight, but his attacker shouted to his comrades, and soon there were a dozen Albans upon him.

"Tie them up. We always need more slaves," the Alban leader ordered, and Grieve soon found his hands bound to his feet. Another man tied Rhona's hands behind her back, then threw her over his shoulder and carried her off.

"Hey. Hey! You can't take her away. That's Lord Ronin's daughter!" he shouted.

The leather-clad leader strode up to him, leaning down so that he might look Grieve in the eye. "She looks too old to be one of his brats to me. Bring the other one."

Doireann was dragged over and thrown to the ground in front of Grieve.

"Who are these two?" the man demanded.

Doireann glared at Grieve. "The boy is the son of Lord Lewis of Myroy. She's Lord Ronin's eldest, and the most unruly of the lot. Good for ransom and not much else."

Grieve met the woman's eye. "At least I still have some honour. I'm not selling out the only people who would take me in to the enemy who killed my family!"

Doireann's eyes burned. "You're a man. You'd never understand." She jerked her head at Rhona. "She will. You'll see. Once all the Albans have had her, stolen her maidenhead and her virtue, she'll agree to anything to make them stop."

"Enough. A lord's maiden daughter is worth more intact. Nobody touches the girl. Not yet." The leader pointed at Doireann. "Get her up, and follow her to this cave. If she cannot show you, kill her."

Two men seized Doireann, ignoring her screaming protests, and took her away.

The leader turned to Grieve and the man still carrying Rhona. "These two…should be held somewhere they cannot escape from. One of the deserted isles we saw on the way. We can return for them later."

"Don't you hurt her!" Grieve shouted.

"And shut that one up," the leader said wearily.

A boot came out of nowhere, colliding with Grieve's head, and blackness embraced him.

Thirty

Rhona's head hadn't hurt this much since she drank a whole jug of wine at Sive's christening. Only she couldn't remember drinking anything this time. Instead, her mouth tasted of blood. She rolled over, and encountered another warm body, but this one didn't move.

She'd fallen asleep with Grieve after making love, and everything afterwards was a bad dream, she told herself, but even she couldn't believe the lie.

"Grieve, where are we?" she asked.

He did not respond, and only then did she

dare to open her eyes. A swollen lump adorned his forehead, crusted with dark blood. But his breathing was even, and his heartbeat felt strong under her hands. Alive, but unconscious. What she wouldn't give for some willow bark now.

Rhona sat up, wincing as her head gave a warning throb. She ignored it. Better to take stock of her surroundings. The light was dim, but still enough to see. They were in a cave, but not of the same stone as Sanctuary. Rhona knew every habitable cave on Rum Isle, and this wasn't one of them. The entrance to this cavern was blocked by a latticework of thin branches, with holes too small for her to fit more than her hand through, yet large enough to see to the larger cavern beyond.

It might not be Sanctuary, but someone called this place home. A pallet in the corner for a bed, and a fire burning peat that smelled like home. A pot bubbled over the fire, but Rhona could not smell what it contained over the smoke from the fire itself.

Her gaze swept the chamber, landing on the light source. It was no candle or lamp, but something else entirely. A swirling blue mist, trapped in what appeared to be a giant platter set against the wall. The thing glowed faintly, and Rhona fancied she saw her own face in the mist before it vanished. Whatever it was, it was magical, which meant that whoever lived here was a powerful witch.

But Rhona was the only witch in the Southern Isles. If there had been another, surely she'd have heard of her. For magic called to magic, and she would know if someone cast a spell near her. For a witch to hide herself and a powerful magical object like this one, she must be a formidable witch indeed. One Rhona did not dare to challenge by magical means.

"Please let us out. I must go home," Rhona said, drawing herself up to her full height.

"We all want to go home, but not everyone gets what they want. The sea wanted to take you from the beach where I found you, but I rescued you from the waves and brought you here. I must keep you two together. The mirror insists." The woman who stepped into view was nothing like Rhona expected. Young and dark-haired, her eyes seemed to contain the night sky.

Rhona shivered. She buried her magic deep inside, where she hoped the woman would never find it.

"Who are you?" the woman asked.

Lost in the woods and taken prisoner by a witch. It was so like one of the tales she and Grieve had swapped that Rhona answered automatically: "I am Gretel, and that's my brother, Hansel. If you don't let us go, our father, Lord Lewis, will not be pleased. Who are you?"

"Once a queen, now a slave, loved by two men, one of whom is now dead and the other is dead to me. I am Briska, now queen of a rock that boasts little more than fearless deer and this horrible stuff called snow."

She sounded mad, though she did not look it. Maybe the magic had made her so.

"You must let us go," Rhona insisted.

"I must do nothing of the sort. The mirror says…the mirror says you must be together. But if you are brother and sister, as you say…then I am cursed!" Briska's eyes glowed blue, the same as the misty platter on the wall. "Bah, I should have known escape was an illusion. You shall not leave here until you break the curse!"

She stormed out, and no amount of calling brought her back.

Rhona slumped to the floor beside Grieve, wishing he would wake up.

Thirty-One

The first thing Grieve became aware of was something cold and wet touching his forehead. Not cold enough to numb the pain, though.

He reached for his sword, but the scabbard was empty. They must have stolen it from him, along with everything else. And Rhona.

Grieve sat up, and saw the most beautiful sight he could have imagined. Rhona's startled face as the wet cloth dangled from her hand, forgotten.

"Are you all right? Did the Albans…did they hurt you?" he asked. He prayed that the leader's promise could be trusted. Who knew with Albans?

"Someone hit me over the back of the head. But nothing else," she said. "You have a bump on your head, too – much worse than mine. Do you know where we are?"

Grieve looked around. "A cave? They didn't say where they were taking us. Somewhere we could not escape from, waiting for a ransom from my father and yours."

Rhona dropped her voice to a whisper. "I told her our father is one and the same, and that we are brother and sister. Hansel and Gretel. They were the first names I could think of. She's a witch, and names are powerful in spells. If she does not know ours, perhaps she will not be able to cast curses at us."

Grieve laughed, then winced as that made his head throb more. "Held captive by a witch, just like a story. Do you have any clever ideas for escape?"

Rhona shook her head. "She keeps saying things about a mirror, and how she is cursed, and we cannot leave until we break the curse. But I know nothing about curses. What about you?"

"I'm no witch, and nor are you. I can shoot a bow, build a house, and lift a sword to defend what is mine. If she's living in a place like this, perhaps I could make a bargain with her. It's worth a try."

He began shouting for the witch.

Rhona tried to hush him, but Grieve only shouted louder.

"Silence, boy!" the dark-haired woman hissed, stalking into the cave like a cat hunting prey. "Or I shall cast a spell on your tongue that will render it unfit for speech, though it may do other things." She smiled, and her hands glowed blue.

Grieve swallowed back the swear words that leaped to his tongue. So the woman was a witch. He would have to be careful, was all, he told himself. "What will it take for you to let my sister and me go?"

This only seemed to anger her further. "Brother and sister. The mirror lies. It will take an abomination before I can release you, and for the mirror to release me from my curse and my exile here."

None of this made any sense to Grieve, but she evidently believed it. He only knew that curses were not his area of expertise. "How would you like to live somewhere better than this cave? If I can't break your curse, maybe I can make your exile more comfortable."

She sniffed. "I do not need a lover, least of all some boy who is supposed to…never mind. I will not do it!" This last was addressed to what appeared to be a mirror on the wall. An image of Grieve and Rhona's faces appeared on it for a moment, before all it showed was the witch's reflection.

A magic mirror. Just like something in a story. And just like in a story, he must somehow trick the witch into letting them go free.

"The men of Myroy have a reputation for our skill with wood. I can build you a beautiful house where you can live. Walls where you can hang your mirror. A bed to sleep on, instead of a pallet on the floor." Grieve had her attention. Now he needed to sweeten the deal. "Much warmer than this cold cave, I promise. Just ask my sister about the other places I have built."

"Oh, he's quite good with wood," Rhona said. "You should have seen the first barn he built by himself when he was just a boy."

Grieve winced. That first barn had been a disaster. But if the witch did not know that…

"What sort of house?" the witch demanded.

Grieve spread his hands wide. "Whatever you like. Point me at the wood, and I shall build you a palace fit for a queen."

Her eyes narrowed. He had her, Grieve was certain.

"A wooden palace. If that is the best I can hope for now…then I accept. You shall build me a palace, and when I am satisfied, you shall go free." The witch nodded, then pointed at Rhona. "But she stays. I will not have…abomination…here."

"No." Grieve folded his arms across his chest. "When the palace is complete, both of us go free."

She eyed him thoughtfully for a long time. "Very well. I shall set you both free, if you give me your solemn vow that you shall never kiss your sister, nor share her bed."

Grieve wanted to laugh, but he did not dare.

"I swear by all I hold dear, by my sister's own life, that I will never kiss my sister, and I will never share her bed." An empty promise, for the only sisters he had died in infancy, and he would not share their grave, nor kiss a corpse if he could help it.

"Good. Then you may start work." The witch unlocked the door, opening it just wide enough for one person to slip through. "But she stays until your work is done."

Grieve squeezed through the gap, then heard it close behind him. "If any harm comes to her, the deal is off."

The witch inclined her head. "Agreed."

"Grieve, I don't trust her," Rhona said behind him.

Grieve didn't trust her, either, but he didn't dare say it. Instead, he ignored Rhona and followed the witch outside to plan out her new palace.

Thirty-Two

Rhona spat out a mouthful of the strange food that burned her mouth. "You are trying to poison me!"

The witch looked affronted. "I feed you the same as I eat. It is not my fault your delicate stomach will not tolerate it." As if to demonstrate, she snatched Rhona's bowl and began to spoon the contents into her own mouth with evident signs of approval. "It is perfectly good venison. I don't know what you are talking about."

Between the burning food, strange flat

sheets of what the witch called bread and the gritty white liquid that the woman called milk but didn't taste like it had come from any kind of cow Rhona had ever met, Rhona wasn't sure how long she would last as the witch's captive. Forcing down every bite of food and then forcing it to stay down was a daily struggle, exacerbated by her need to hide her magic deep inside, too, lest the witch sense it.

Yet the more Rhona saw of this witch, the more she thought the woman was mad. She spent hours talking to the misty platter that looked nothing like the bronze mirrors on the islands, yet the witch insisted on calling a mirror.

More than once, Rhona had seen her own face in the mist, and Grieve's, too. She fancied she'd seen the mirror show that blissful night she and Grieve had spent together in Sanctuary, once or twice, but the witch shouted at it that such things were an abomination before storming out. Without the witch present, all the mist did was swirl, without showing pictures.

Rhona barely saw Grieve, who wasn't even

allowed to sleep in the same cavern as her any more. Only when the witch was fast asleep did Grieve dare to approach the door to Rhona's prison. His hands were too big to fit through the bars, so she had to shove her fingers through to feel his touch again.

"Kill her in her sleep, and let's leave together," Rhona begged on the first night.

But Grieve had shaken his head. "I gave my word, and I will not break it. If she dishonours our deal, then I will have no mercy, but for now, stay here where you will be safe. There is no way off this island – there are no boats at all. Unless I can build one or persuade one to land here, the witch is our best chance of finding a way home. I'm working as fast as I can, but I cannot build a house in a day, so you must have patience. I swear to you, I will get you home."

The witch had awoken then, putting an end to any further conversation. "Get away from her!" she'd shouted, swatting at Grieve with a broom.

So Rhona fought her frustration, finding reserves of patience she didn't know she had.

Most of her days, she spent sitting in the corner of her cell, wondering what her sisters were doing at home. Whether her father had arrived home yet. And what had happened to Doireann.

Finally, one night Grieve came in so exhausted, he flopped right down on his pallet and didn't seem to want to get up again. "Tomorrow, I shall finish my work, and you can move your things from here to your new home," he told the witch. Lifting his head so that he might meet Rhona's eyes, he added, "And then tomorrow, we shall go free."

"Yes. Good," the witch said, intent on stirring the pot over the fire. It undoubtedly contained something intended to burn through the roof of Rhona's mouth. What she wouldn't give for some normal bread, or a piece of roast pork, but the only animals the witch had were deer, or at least that's all the meat she used.

The next morning, Rhona washed with the small bucket of water in her cell, and attempted to re-braid her hair. Today, she would be free.

The witch wandered in and out of the cave,

as usual, muttering to herself or the misty mirror. Rhona paid her little attention until the woman dropped the pot she'd been holding with a clang.

"It will not happen! Incest is against nature!" she shouted at the mirror.

Rhona peered through the bars of her prison. The mirror showed her and Grieve, locked in a lovers' embrace. The image brought a blush to her cheeks as she watched her own image arch her back and cry out in joy. What she wouldn't give to do that with Grieve again. When they were home, and wed, she promised herself.

"Better to kill them than let him defile her so. Now, before it is too late!" The witch seized a knife and raced out of the cave.

Rhona shouted for the witch to come back, but the woman never heard.

She was headed out to kill Grieve.

She would have to get through Rhona first.

Rhona threw her weight against the bars, trying to pry them apart wide enough to let her through. To no avail – the latticework was too firmly fixed to come apart in her hands.

But it was wood, and wood burned.

Would it matter if the witch knew about Rhona's magic? By day's end, one of them would be dead. As long as the witch didn't get to Grieve before Rhona could warn him.

Her hands were already bleeding from her fruitless attack on the door, so the spell was barely a thought away. She pressed her bloodied hands to the wood, leaving two handprints as she backed away.

Rhona pressed her back against the wall, as far from the door as she could get, and commanded the wood to burn.

The handprints ignited, leaving blackened holes in the lattice, as flames licked hungrily at the edges. Within moments, the whole door was ablaze, and it only took a few minutes before the whole thing was reduced to ashes.

Rhona hitched up her skirts above the embers, and marched through the still-smoking remains of her prison.

"I'm coming for you, bitch," she said.

And if the witch had hurt Grieve, her death was going to be slow and painful.

Thirty-Three

Grieve heard the approaching footsteps, but he didn't look up until he'd finished hammering the shingle into place.

"Almost done!" he called. "Three more to go, and then I'll climb down to show you around!"

He'd be done already if one of the shingles hadn't split overnight, bringing down part of the roof. But that was the thing about wood. It might look perfect at first, and fit just fine with all the rest, but weeks or months or sometimes even years later, the fault deep inside would start to show, and it would crack, to the detriment of all around it. Much like people, really.

He shot a furtive glance at the witch. She was barely more than a girl herself, of an age with Rhona and Bedelia, which meant he had to tread carefully lest his clumsy tongue land him in trouble again. His care seemed to have paid off, for the witch appeared pleased with his progress on her house. Well, she had, until now. The frown on her face sent out silent alarm bells, warning him to rethink his every word before he spoke.

He hammered the last shingle into place. "Would you like to see inside your new palace, mistress?" he called from his perch on the roof. Out of reach, he thought, then wondered just how far she could cast a spell. If it was like an archer firing arrows, then he was well in range, and nowhere he stood would be safe.

Grieve climbed down the ladder and rounded the cottage. She stood in the same spot, her frown even deeper.

Grieve strode past her and opened the door. He bowed extravagantly. "Your new palace,

Your Majesty."

She almost smiled, lifting her head regally as she stepped forward.

"Get away from her! She means to kill you!"

Rhona raced into view, shouting at him and the witch.

"What?" Grieve stared at the witch, as she stared at him. He took a step back, just in case.

Rhona slowed to a halt, panting. "She said she was going to kill you." Her eyes widened in panic. "Oh, no, you don't!"

A gust of wind blew Grieve almost off his feet, it was so powerful. The same gale had pinned the witch against the door, though she struggled against it. In her hand was a curved knife with a green stone blade, like nothing Grieve had ever seen before.

The witch's hands glowed blue.

"Don't you dare touch him, you bitch!" For a moment, it looked like Rhona held a handful of flames, before she drew her hand back and threw the missile. Whatever it was, it splashed at the witch's feet, engulfing her boots in roaring flame.

She screamed and ran inside the house,

slamming the door behind her.

Rhona followed, raising her arms.

"Move, Grieve," she said. She waved her hand in his direction, and this time it seemed the very air lifted him up and deposited him at her feet. "Now, burn, bitch," she said, gritting her teeth. She turned her hands palm up, lifting them as though raising an imaginary host to heaven. But what she raised was more hellish than divine, as the house he'd painstakingly built went up in a whoosh of flame.

"Rhona!" He couldn't seem to say anything else. Couldn't think. Rhona, a witch? How?

A burst of blue light erupted from the house as the roof collapsed, so blinding they both had to turn away. It took a moment for Grieve to regain his sight, and when he did, half the house was gone, collapsed in on itself and the witch's body, no doubt, for the woman's screaming had stopped.

Rhona's breast heaved. She bent down to pick up the knife, which had magically landed at her feet.

Grieve's blood ran cold. Magically, indeed. She'd just killed a woman. What else could

Rhona do?

Perhaps the witch wasn't the one he had to fear after all.

He rose onto unsteady feet. If he'd been frightened of her before…she terrified him now. A woman who could command fire didn't need him to protect her. She didn't need anyone's protection – she was a force of nature all by herself.

Rhona threw her arms around his neck and kissed him. It took him a stunned moment before he could force his mouth open to return her kiss.

It wasn't enough. She sensed that something was wrong, and pulled away.

Tears glimmered in her eyes. "I'm sorry. I couldn't let her kill you."

Grieve didn't know what to say. It didn't seem right to accept her apology, not when she was sorry for saving his life, but thanking her didn't seem right, either. Instead, he said, "How will we get home now?"

She turned and surveyed the water. "We'll need a boat." She closed her eyes and bit her lip.

Grieve felt a breeze spring up, nowhere near as powerful as the one that had carried him, but he knew it came from the same source. Rhona. A witch so powerful she commanded the elements.

Fire, air…would she part the sea so that they might walk home? Anything seemed possible.

Never in his life had he felt so small, so insignificant. Not even when Bedelia rejected him.

He was nothing next to Rhona. No one. For she deserved some great hero, a man of power and wealth and courage, while what was he? Some lord's younger son, who owned little more than his clothes and weapons, which he was competent with, but no more than that. He worked wood, but she could turn a week's work into ash with a wave of her hand.

Grieve fancied he heard voices.

"We should try in the lee of Nimbanmore. Good fishing there."

Fishermen? He glanced around, but saw no one but themselves.

"There's a curse on Nimbanmore, my

grandmother says. No one who goes there ever comes back."

This voice was softer, as though whispered on the wind.

"We're not going to land there, just fish offshore. Hey, what's that smoke? Seems there's someone on the island."

That's how she was doing it, Grieve realised. Stealing the sound of their words somehow.

"Where are they?" Grieve asked.

Rhona opened her eyes and pointed. "In the lee of this island. Nimbanmore, which explains why we are the only ones here. There is a curse here, an ancient one, laid on the lake at the top of the mountain. I can feel it faintly now, but it won't hurt us. Not if we can get off this island soon." She waved her hand. "They will have no choice but to come to us. The wind in every other direction will send them onto the rocks."

Grieve couldn't believe what he was hearing. "You're going to kill some innocent fishermen?"

She tilted her head to the side and smiled.

"They are hardly innocent. What man is? But no, I do not intend to kill them. If they cannot sail in this wind, they may wreck their boat, but they are Islanders and fisherman. The fishermen of Rum Isle survive gales far worse than this. They will come to the beach here, and take us home. You'll see."

It seemed to take forever before the boat landed on the beach, and the men aboard hailed them. Rhona explained who they were and how they needed a ride home, for which she would happily pay the men to make up for their lost catch.

This was Lady Rhona, Ronin's daughter, not the frightened girl she'd been for the last week in the witch's prison. How much of that had been real, and how much a pretence? Grieve truly didn't know the woman at his side at all. Witch, woman, wonder…but she could never be his wife. He wanted to worship her, not ask her what was for dinner.

Exactly as Rhona had foretold, Grieve found himself beside her on the fishing boat, headed home to Rum Isle. Standing beside the woman who held his heart, when he would never have hers.

Lord Ronin wept when he saw Rhona, and he couldn't seem to stop thanking Grieve for bringing her home. He either didn't hear or chose to ignore Grieve's protestations that he'd done nothing, and embraced him like a son.

Doireann was dead, murdered by the Albans, and Ronin had feared Rhona had suffered a similar fate.

"If not for you, I would have lost everything," Lord Ronin said with an enormous sniffle.

He still had his house, all the supplies in

Sanctuary, and three of his daughters unharmed because of their early retreat to the caves, Grieve thought but didn't say as the three girls lined up to hug Rhona and drop an awkward curtsey each in his direction, at their father's command.

Grieve wanted to turn and run right out of the house, then maybe take up an axe and vent his frustration on a dozen trees, but Rhona would not approve. So he stayed and tried his best to look the part of the hero, though he felt like the opposite.

"And I would like to say that Rum Isle will always be home to the man who saved my daughter. May you always be here to keep her safe, for I am sure Rhona will want to marry you as soon as possible, and I give my hearty blessing to you both!" Ronin said with a watery smile.

"Father…" The warning in her tone made Grieve want to run more than ever.

The one woman he wanted for his wife, who could never be his.

"There's my boy! They say you've saved one girl, and I could ask no less than a hero for the quest I have in mind." Father entered the hall, arms spread wide to embrace his son.

"Father, I need to speak to you," Grieve muttered as his father hugged him.

Lord Lewis clapped him on the back. "Let's leave them to their family reunion, so we can have one of our own." He led the way into the yard.

Grieve went further, walking all the way down to the river. He knew Rhona would hear him if she wished it, but perhaps her father might not.

"Father, I saved no one. Lady Rhona saved herself. She is…" Grieve lowered his voice to a whisper. "She is a witch. She has power over the elements of fire and air. I saw her reduce a house to ashes in minutes. Surely her father must know, for how could she keep that hidden from her own family? Yet he seems to believe I saved her, instead of the other way around!"

Father scratched his chin. "It always was a mystery that Lady Blanid fell pregnant so quickly after her wedding, for she was not one to take her husband to bed earlier than needs must. Especially after…well, Lord Ronin nearly lost her to Alban raiders, too. Her sister saved her, or so 'tis said. I always wondered how a slip of a girl could take on a whole party of raiders like that. If what you say is true, then your girl must be the sister's daughter. But still Ronin's, for he would not have acknowledged her if she were not."

"I don't care whose daughter she is!" Grieve exploded, struggling to keep his voice quiet. "She's a witch. A sorceress. A woman who can burn me where I stand with a wave of her hand. I cannot marry her!"

Father stared. "She seems a lovely enough girl. If you can but keep from provoking her, there is little to worry about on that account."

"I'm not worried for me! I'm worried for her! What do I have to give her? I'm not fit to lick the ash from her boots! I'm no hero – I'm no one. She deserves far more than anything I can give her." Grieve gazed at his father, begging him to understand. "You should have sent me to war first, not here, so I might be a war hero, at least. Someone with something to offer her."

"So you like the girl, but she thinks you're not good enough, hmm?"

Grieve shook his head. "I do not know what she thinks. I…she…when she kissed me, it seemed like she liked me…but I…"

"You will not be the first man who did not feel ready for marriage. Even I hesitated once…but the right lady will have her own way of making her heart known. Perhaps it is best to take you away from here for a while, until you are ready." Lord Lewis held Grieve's gaze, so he could not look away. "The Alban king has sent a letter that is tantamount to a declaration of war. He demands Lord Angus' eldest daughter and heir, Lady Portia, as bride to one of his sons."

Grieve spluttered. "We can't give her to Alba. Handing over Isla to them is tantamount to giving them all the Southern Isles."

Father grinned. "So you do understand a bit of strategy, after all. Yes. Giving them the girl is to give them everything. But there's more. The Council sent an envoy to the Viken king, asking for him to honour our alliance and send troops to fight the Albans when they come.

Lady Portia…will be the price of that alliance. A marriage bargain between her and the Viken prince, when he lands on our shores." He cleared his throat. "But she must be kept safe, never be without a bodyguard at all times. Lady Portia is no witch. She needs protection, and the Council agrees. That's why we all had to send a member of our family to form her bodyguard. I need Mahon on Myroy, so I must send you."

Leave Rhona? The very thought cleaved Grieve's heart in two. "Father…"

"Fools like Calum are sending suitors for her hand, seeing this as a chance to take Isla for their own. But any man who marries her is doomed to die, if he is not either the Alban prince or the Viken one. The alliance will be written in her maiden's blood, or her husband's lifeblood. I need one man among them who can lead them, forge them into the bodyguard the girl needs. Before she shoots the lot of them. She's a keen archer, I've heard." Once again, Father's eyes captured Grieve's. "You are the only man I trust. That is why I sent you here first. If your heart is here, then there is no way you will lose it to Lady Portia. And when you return, you will be a war hero – Lady Portia's valiant protector. Surely Lady Rhona cannot turn her nose up at that."

Grieve closed his eyes. "What sort of girl is Lady Portia?"

"She is her father's daughter, and her mother's, too. Passionate to a fault, but she knows her duty. Catriona married for love, but she also married the only man who could lead us. Angus says Portia will do the same. Your job is to make sure she gets a choice, though my money's on her picking the Viken prince."

"Very well, Father. I shall go to Isla. For how long?"

Father shrugged. "Until the war is over, and the girl marries her prince. War is a messy business. No one can be sure how long it will last."

Grieve bowed his head. "Then we must tell Lord Ronin, and Rhona."

Father grinned. "Want me to bring a bucket of water to put the fire out?"

Grieve wished he could laugh, but there was nothing funny about deserting Rhona now.

She might not need him, but that didn't change how much he cared about her. If war was coming to the isles, the Albans would return in even greater numbers, and she could be caught unawares again. But he'd been as good as useless, anyway. Better to go to Lady Portia, and be useless among a dozen other men, hoping they would be enough to protect the girl.

Grieve took a deep breath and marched up to the house. This would not go well.

Thirty-Five

"Rhona, wait!" Grieve called, but Rhona didn't.

She intended to set fire to something and watch it burn to ashes before she'd do anything for Grieve again. One moment he was ready to marry her, and the next he intended to head off to guard some girl on a faraway island? Who was this Lady Portia to him, anyway?

She wanted to run into the woods and hide where he'd never find her, but the sea was closer. Something on the beach would surely burn. But the tide was in, licking at the sand,

and the rock the seals liked to sun themselves on was now surrounded by dark water. Rhona didn't care. She summoned a gust of wind to carry her to that rock, where no one could reach her until she willed it.

"Rhona, come back! Please," Grieve said, as he slowed at the water's edge. "I have to do this."

"You have to protect Portia, do you? And why is she so special?" Rhona reached for the beach, for the tiny specks of dried seaweed and sawdust between the sand, and ignited them. The shore lit up like a grassfire.

Grieve jumped back onto a rock. "She's Lord Angus's daughter. His eldest. The heir to Isla."

The fire died for lack of fuel. Rhona cursed. "So? What's Isla to you? Why kiss me, make love to me if you intend to go off and marry this other woman so you can be lord of her island instead? Is Rum Isle not good enough for you? Or is it me? I am not good enough for you, now you know I am a witch and a bastard."

Grieve shook his head. "It is I who is not

good enough for Rum Isle, or you. You are…a powerful sorceress, who will one day be the lady of prosperous Rum Isle, able to protect this place without needing a husband. As for Angus' daughter…Lady Portia and the lordship of all the isles is as far beyond me as the very heavens above. The Albans want her as a wife to one of their princes, and I have no doubt the Vikens will offer for her as well."

"Women are not prizes to be carried away like the spoils of war," Rhona snapped.

Grieve sobered. "No, you are not. And nor is she, which is why I must go. Alba will not have her without a fight."

Rhona swallowed. "Is she more important to you than I am?"

"No," he admitted. "She is perhaps the most important woman in the isles right now, because with her claim to Isla comes a chance at kingship, or so the Council says. I should want to defend her with my life because if Alba gets her, then they will conquer us all, and no one will be safe. I would give anything to stay here and marry you like I promised. But war is coming, and I am honour bound to fight and defend what is ours, as is every man of the isles. And you…you are not mine. Not yet. I don't deserve you. You saved us both on that island, and you have no need of me as your defender. When war comes to Rum Isle, as it will to Isla, I know you will save your family without me. My place is where I am most needed, and my father says it is on Isla, guarding the last of the Three Little Pigs."

It was Rhona's turn to laugh. "You mean THAT Lady Portia of the little pigs tale? She cannot be much to look at, if she is likened to a pig. I imagine she is kept cloistered like some princess in a tower, waiting for her prince to come and claim her."

"Perhaps. I do not know, for I have never seen the girl. My father says that she has inherited her father's instinct for politics, and that she is fond of archery. Perhaps he is sending me to her to be her bowyer and archery instructor, more than her bodyguard. I will not be alone, either — all the lords are sending men to guard her. It will not be forever. Only until the war against the Albans is over, or the girl chooses a husband."

Rhona jumped off her rock, splashing through the shallows to shore. She was too tired to use magic, and too tired to argue any more. Grieve was right, though it pained her to admit it. "Fight with honour, and don't let the Albans touch her. And when your duty is done, come home to me. I will wait for you."

Grieve ventured onto the sand, crossing the distance between them without hesitation. "Truly, I do not deserve you. But I will do as you command, for I live in hope." He kissed her, the moment stretching as Rhona tasted longing, desire and duty in that kiss. Longing and desire wanted to continue, but it was duty that ended it. "Farewell, my lady. If it is our fate to meet again on these shores, then I will marry you."

Then he turned and was gone. Rhona waited until he was out of sight before she sank to her knees and let the tears flow. If fate didn't bring him back to her, she'd burn that bitch's bones to ash. Just like the witch. And every Alban who thought to stand between her and vengeance.

Thirty-Six

Rhona didn't return to the house until she knew they'd sailed away. Her eyes were probably red from crying, but no one would notice if she kept her head down. If her father asked, she could say they were tears of grief for Doireann.

She entered the Great Hall, expecting to find it empty.

Of course, it wasn't.

Lord Lewis lifted his cup to her. "My son tells me you are a witch, Lady Rhona. We haven't had one here on the isles in many years. We may need your help to drive off the Albans if it comes to war."

Father slammed his cup down. "No, man, you may send your sons to war, but leave my daughter be. Women protect their homes, with force if need be, but they do not go to war. We need her here at home."

"You're holding her here, just like you did to Brigid. I don't know what you did, but no matter how much she wanted to marry me, she stayed here with you! You had a wife. You didn't need her!" Lewis said, pouring himself another cup.

"Lady Brigid loved her sister, not me. Maybe not even you, either. I could not have kept her here against her will. The woman took on Alban raiders thrice, with not a survivor among them. If she were here, Doireann would not have died." Father peered into his cup.

"Doireann was a traitorous bitch who deserved to die. The Albans only spared her on Scitis because she promised to tell them the location of the riches of Rum Isle. They killed her here because she could not lead them to

Sanctuary." Rhona folded her arms across her chest. "I would have killed her, had they not knocked me unconscious before I could. I heard enough to damn her before they did. My mother would not have protected her."

Father peered blearily at her. "Did Blanid tell you? She was the only one who knew, except Brigid and me. I was too drunk on my wedding night to know the difference – drunk because I couldn't bear to see the bride I loved flinch every time I touched her, after what those bastards did to her. The second time, I knew she wasn't my wife, but, God forgive me, I lay with her anyway. She said she would do what her sister couldn't…to pretend…and I did. Blanid claimed you as hers, and I knew you were mine. Brigid wanted to give me a son, though, so we tried again…and again, but the babies did not live long enough, and then, nor did she. And Blanid…it took years before she would tolerate my touch, but she promised her sister she'd try…but we never had a son. When she died, I swore I'd never lie with another woman, and be grateful for the children I had. Doireann was a widow, I wanted her to be a nurse to my girls, but she refused to live under my roof unless we were married. So I took another vow, but she was never a wife to me. My daughters are enough."

"You mean you knew I was a bastard?" Rhona asked.

"You are my daughter, the heir to Rum Isle, until I say otherwise, and there are no bastards under this roof. I swore to Brigid on her deathbed, and I keep my oaths." Father rose. "I will hear no more of this matter. As the Lady of Rum Isle, you will protect it as your mother would."

Rhona slumped into a seat and poured herself a cup of wine. "Yes, Father."

Father nodded, took his leave of Lord Lewis, and left.

"Now how did he know you were thinking of running away to Isla, and Grieve?" Lord Lewis asked.

Rhona glared at him. "I most certainly was not!" she lied.

Lord Lewis sipped from his cup, then set it down. "My son tells me you are fond of stories. May I tell you one? One I do not think even my son knows, though he will, in time."

Rhona inclined her head. "Go on."

"Have you heard the story of the Three Little Pigs?" At Rhona's nod, he continued, "And do you remember who saves the little girls?"

"Their nurse," Rhona said slowly. "Like Candace saved my sisters."

"What if I told you it was the wolf?"

Rhona eyed him. "Then I would think you a fool, Lord Lewis, which my father tells me is not true. But if you have had as much to drink as my father, perhaps it is the wine talking."

Lewis laughed. "Wine does not talk, but it does make men talk. Too much, sometimes. Like the day Lord Angus told me about his little wolf, the prince we have all pinned our hopes on." His shrewd eyes peered at her over the rim of his cup. Lord Lewis was as sober as Rhona herself.

"What if I told you Lord Angus took a Viken fosterling, a young prince, his blood as royal as both the king's and the crown prince, as a favour to his father? And on the day of the feast meant to welcome the boy, Lord

Angus's own daughters went missing. Little Portia, the leader of the three, wanted to go swimming, she said, but her nurse said no. So when the nurse wasn't looking, she led the girls out of their father's house and down to a pool she'd heard the boys speak of… And when no one could find the girls, the young prince went searching. He found the girls in the mud, and raised the alarm so the nurse came running. Two girls came when the nurse called, but little Portia refused. He waded into the middle of that mud in his best clothes, heedless of the damage he did to them, and coaxed her out. A different man might have thrown the little girl over his shoulder and carried her out, but that boy offered her his hand and they walked out of the woods together, hand in hand."

"Why are you telling me this?" Rhona demanded.

Lewis smiled. "My son adores you, Lady Rhona, and I know he will return to Rum Isle for you. Much like I know the Viken Wolf Prince is in love with Lady Portia, and he will return to claim her. My son will do his duty, for he is honour-bound to uphold his oath. I knew your mother, and she would never desert her family, not for love or her own happiness. She would fight to the death to protect those she loved. Including you."

Rhona's eyes blazed. "Are you telling me to stay home, like a good little girl?"

To Lord Lewis' credit, he did not back down. "No, Lady Rhona. I am suggesting you do everything within your power to protect Rum Isle and its people, including yourself. For the only man who can end the war against Alba is that Viken prince, and until he arrives, you are the best Rum Isle has. Just as I am all Myroy has, and Grieve must keep Portia safe for the Viken. We all must endure until our allies arrive. But that doesn't mean we won't fight. On the contrary. We will be defending our homes, more fiercely than any Alban raider can imagine." Lord Lewis rose from his seat and bowed. "Lady Rhona, I would hope you burn every Alban you see, before he even reaches the shore of your lovely isle. I have no doubt you will make your mother proud." He headed off.

Rhona sipped from her cup, deep in

thought. She wasn't sure what to think, or to do. Too many revelations in too short a time. And yet…somehow, she thought it would all turn out all right in the end. How, she did not know, but all the best stories did, and hers…would be the best she could make it. Making her mother proud did have a lovely ring to it.

Thirty-Seven

When war came to Rum Isle, her people came to Sanctuary. So it was, and so it always would be. After the initial attack, though, the Albans had left no garrison on Rum Isle, so most of her people had returned to their homes. All except Lord Ronin's family, for their home had been burned along with the Albans and their boats. Rhona had learned her lesson – after the first attack, she'd burned the boats at sea. No Alban would set foot on her shore while she lived.

There had been whispers at first, until her

father insisted that his daughter had Lady Brigid's blood in her veins and the magic that ran with it, and she would defend the island alongside its men. After watching what she could do, the men heartily embraced this idea, and the whispers ceased.

So Sanctuary echoed with emptiness, until a boat was spotted approaching Rum Isle.

The watchmen reported this to Rhona, while the people of Rum Isle filled Sanctuary again.

"We have visitors," Rhona announced to her family. Her sisters huddled closer together, looking fearful. "Don't worry, I shall see them off shortly."

Father caught her arm. "Don't go out there alone. I shall come with you. Remember what happened to Doireann."

Rhona gently pulled out of his grasp. "Doireann got what she deserved, luring Albans to our home. As will our latest intruders. Don't worry, Father. They will tell no tales once I am finished with them."

But Father would not be dissuaded. He buckled on his sword and shouldered his crossbow. "Once we both are finished with them. I am not so old that I cannot defend Rum Isle."

Blowing out a frustrated breath, she waited for him to lead the way out of the cave and onto the ridge, where he took up his accustomed spot behind a boulder that was just the right height to rest his crossbow on.

Two figures beached a coracle, before one climbed the rocks above the beach and started shouting. Shouting her name.

Rhona swore. "It's Lord Lewis. With another man."

Her heart leaped. Was it finally time to stop hiding, and start fighting?

"I have a proposition for you!" Lord Lewis bellowed.

Rhona squinted at the second man. Only one man had a proposition she might want to hear, and Lord Lewis' companion did not look like Grieve.

"Stay here and defend the girls, Father. I will speak to him."

Bless the man, he looked like he wanted to argue. As though two men would be any match for Rhona and her magic.

She bit her lip. Sparks erupted from her fingers. "I will be fine, Father."

He nodded. "And I will keep them in my sights."

She let the wind carry away the sound of her footsteps, so that the men would not hear her approach. Lord Lewis's companion dressed like a man of Isla, with a coracle to match, but no Islander ever wore a sealskin so fine over Isla wool, except perhaps Lord Angus. Lord Angus was closer to her father's age than this man, who could not be older than thirty. And Lord Angus had no sons, least of all this giant.

Lord Lewis shouted his offer again.

"I'm already betrothed, and not to that beast of a man." Rhona stepped out of hiding.

She'd surprised the Viken, for that's what he must be. Was this the man Lewis had promised would come to their aid?

Lewis' impassive face told her nothing. Instead, he gestured for the Viken to speak.

He inclined his head with what appeared to be genuine courtesy. "I am no beast, lady." The rumble of his delightfully deep voice said otherwise, as he continued, "I am Rudolf Vargssen, Prince of Viken. I have come from my cousin, King Reidar, to cast the Albans out of the Southern Isles." His eyes flashed with something like battle-fire.

One man's fire would only go so far.

Rhona dismissed him with a flick of her fingers. "Just you and old Lewis here? You have no chance, Prince of Viken. Not without an army that can match the Albans."

A faint smile curved his lips. The Viken liked a challenge. "I have three ships." Rudolf pointed.

Still Lewis said nothing. Did he think she was a politician like Lady Portia, able to read men and their true intentions before they knew themselves? Lady Portia dealt in subtleties. Rhona did not.

"Is this the wolf we are waiting for?" Rhona demanded.

Lewis inclined his head. "He is."

She wanted to breathe out a sigh of relief, but the Viken had his eyes on her. Instead, she inspected him right back. "What is your stake, Prince of Viken? What do you get out of saving the Southern Isles?"

For just a moment, Rudolf looked lost, like a boy looked out through his eyes. Then the moment was gone and he stood as stoic as before, almost as though she'd imagined it. But she hadn't.

"He wants Lady Portia," Lewis supplied.

Good luck, Viken. If Grieve was to be believed, and he usually was, Lady Portia would be no easy conquest. She might not be a witch, but she had her own weapons. If this man sought to bully Lady Portia into a marriage she did not desire, Rhona would defend her alongside Grieve and the others. "Lady Portia is no prize, like the women of other lands. She is the Lady of Isla, and if she does not like you, may heaven help you, for no one else will."

She expected him to defend his title, his suitability as a suitor. His right to conquer a woman.

What she didn't expect was his laughter.

He wiped his eyes and shrugged. "Portia liked me well enough before I left. If she likes me still...well, I guess we shall see. As long as the lady is safe, I will be satisfied."

She stared at him for a long moment. He spoke the truth, she was sure of it. And that look in his eyes…yearning, that's what it was. But for Portia or her claim?

Slowly, Rhona said, "She is safe enough. My betrothed guards her with his life."

Rudolf relaxed just the slightest bit. Relieved. Rhona bridled. If he dismissed Grieve and his men so easily, she would give him a piece of her mind.

"My son has sent word?" Lewis asked eagerly, interrupting her train of thought.

Rudolf would keep, Rhona swore, as she answered, "When he can. His letters are carried in secret and left in a place only he and I know. The lady lives, and so does he."

Lewis' grin was positively devilish. "How goes the hiding, Lady Rhona? Are your sisters sick of fish yet?"

Rhona turned her glare on Lewis. "They complain constantly. The sooner this war ends, the better." If she could play a part in it, it would be over much sooner.

The two men exchanged a glance.

"Would you like to help with the war, Lady Rhona?" Rudolf ventured. He almost sounded like he wanted her to refuse.

Fat chance of that. "My father will not approve."

Lewis laughed. "Old fool. He thinks my son should save you, for what man would follow a hero who got himself saved by a maiden?"

No, her father worried about her. Needlessly. "Something of that sort." It was Grieve she worried about. If she went to war…Grieve agreed with her father. He would not forgive her for going to war, when it was his place to fight.

Lewis jerked his head at Rudolf. "We can blame the victory on the Viken. I'm sure he won't mind."

The Viken looked affronted. A proud prince, this one. "I prefer to fight my own battles, but I am not such a fool as to refuse the help of an ally. There are shieldmaidens among my people, Lord Lewis's late mother among them, who fight alongside their men. If you can assist my army…"

He didn't believe she could. Then he was a

fool.

Rhona bit her lip, and the bush behind Lewis burst into flame.

He yelped and ran down to the water, but she sent the fire racing after him, blistering the very sands to glass until the sea steamed around him. "I told you! This witch can burn anything! With her on your side, you can't help but win!"

Witch. Rhona didn't like that word. She fought to find more that would burn in the sand at Lewis's feet, but all she found was a clump of seaweed that sent up a satisfying cloud of steam. She would not help this man conquer her countrywoman. They were Islanders, not Vikens or Albans who used women like slaves. And Lewis was a traitor who deserved to die with them.

There was a whump as Rudolf fell to his knees on the sand. "Lady Rhona, I beg you to help me free the Southern Isles from the invaders. I will give you anything you ask."

It was so easy to say no, but then she would be as much a fool as Lewis. If this man with his three ships prevailed, he would face Grieve.

And Grieve would die to protect Portia.

Rhona took a deep breath. "I want all I've ever wanted. My husband. Free him from his oath to Portia, so that he can come home and marry me."

The Viken bowed his head. Understanding lit his eyes. This man had known love, too. Time would tell if it was for Lady Portia, and whether she shared his love. And Rhona would be at his side when it did, to protect her own people if it came to it. Damn Grieve and his stupid pride. It was time for this war to end, and this wolfish Viken had the power to do it. With her help.

Rhona took a deep breath. "What would you have me burn first?"

"Myroy Isle, and every other island where Albans seek to hide," Lewis said, splashing out of the sea. He shrugged. "What? I'm the Lord of Myroy. I can burn it if I want to." Lewis produced a jug from under his cloak and lifted it in a toast: "To winning this damned war!" He drank deeply.

Rudolf held out his hand. "Do we have an accord?"

If Rudolf was to live up to his name, he would have to win this war. Perhaps Grieve need never know the part she'd played. Rhona placed her hand in his. "We do, Wolf Prince."

His fingers closed around hers with a delicacy she had not expected. If it weren't for Grieve, she might actually like this Viken. Perhaps Portia would, too.

But it was too early to think of such things. First, she had a war to fight, and win.

Thirty-Eight

Rhona had seen death and destruction enough for a dozen lifetimes. She'd seen men die screaming, burning, and she'd enjoyed it. Prince Rudolf was the only man who dared stand at her side, or anywhere near her, and he did his best to arrange his face into an expression of battle-hardened watchfulness. But he was still a man, and sometimes he'd feared, sometimes he'd despaired, but more often he cheered in triumph as their growing army won yet another victory over the diminishing Alban army.

For he might be a Viken, but the Islanders treated him like one of their own. What Lord Lewis had told her was true – Rudolf had grown up on the Isles, Rhona had learned, fostered by Lord Angus, though none had known he was a prince then. And he'd fought alongside many of them as a boy, which even Rhona had to admit made him one of them. For who but an Islander fought to defend the Southern Isles?

Albans ran at the sight of him, for his reputation flew faster than an eagle. He slaughtered and burned everything in his path, they screamed, little knowing it wasn't Rudolf at all they feared, but Rhona herself. And she didn't slaughter and burn everything. Just Albans. But she let the stories spread, as stories always did. She laughed when her own people called her the Viken witch, thinking she had arrived with Rudolf. Better that they believe a lie than that she was one of their own. The men of Rum Isle knew the truth, but they kept their lady's secrets. As did Rudolf.

Twice Rhona had seen Rudolf's spirits rise at the sight of a red-haired woman on Isla, only for them to be dashed the moment the women opened their mouths. They were Lady Portia's sisters, identical in all but name and disposition. Rudolf had two of the Little Pigs, but he really wanted Number Three. Who was kept captive in a castle the Albans had dared to build on Council Isle.

When he'd heard that, he'd ordered them to ride without rest until they arrived at the loch. No one had dared argue with the hard Viken. Not even Rhona. This war had gone on too long – they all wanted it to be over.

The sisters rode with Rhona all the way to Loch Findlugan, which made the men keep their distance. They needn't have – the pregnant one, Arlie, spent most of the journey describing the gowns she wanted to make for Rhona. If it hadn't been raining, Rhona didn't doubt the woman would have had a needle in hand, making a start on the first gown while she rode. Rhona had half a mind to take her up on the offer. It would be nice to have a new gown again.

Lina had little to say, except when answering her sister's questions about the cloth bales in Lord Angus' storerooms. But Rhona could feel her eyes everywhere, sizing up the army and the land and everything they encountered. No doubt taking stock so that she might report to her husband, Lord Angus' steward.

Rudolf stayed away when the women were with her, which suited Rhona fine. Every time he looked at them, his eyes burned with a desire that forced him to look away. He burned for Lady Portia, hotter than any blaze Rhona had kindled. If Portia refused him…Rhona wasn't sure what he'd do. That's why she would see this through to the end. Prince Rudolf, the Wolf Prince of Viken, as he was now known, had fought too long and too hard to just give up, and with an army at his back, Rhona might be all that stood between him and Portia, if the girl refused him.

But Rhona would stand, for this war would be all for naught if Portia was forced into a marriage against her will. For the women of the Southern Isles fought for freedom as much as their men, and Rhona would not yield.

When Rudolf sent his envoys across the

loch, against Rhona's advice, she considered returning to her tent, not wanting to see if the Albans opened fire on the two helpless women in the tiny boat. But something within her could not turn away, so she stayed. A whisper of magic sent a breeze behind the boat, speeding it to the castle, then swirling back to her, carrying the voices of those inside.

But not the words she wanted to hear.

For the first time in years, she heard Grieve's voice again: "I don't care if they're her sisters or not. If they are soldiers in disguise, then they die on our swords, but if they truly are Lady Portia's sisters, then we'll send them up to the tower with her, where they'll be safe. God knows she could do with the company of a woman again. Keeping her amused is more than I have the wit or energy for, I fear."

Grieve's loyalties had shifted, as Rhona had known they would. He served Lady Portia now. He'd forgotten Rhona had ever existed.

Rhona bowed her head, wiping away a tear before anyone could see it.

"What is it? What's wrong? Is it Portia?" Rudolf seized her shoulders, forgetting in his panic who she was.

Rhona eyed him coldly. "Your Lady Portia is in the tower, soon to be joined by her sisters. So safe her guards have little to do but amuse her."

Rudolf's breath whooshed out of him. "Thank the heavens for that. For a moment, I thought…"

He remembered himself and released her.

"Forgive me, Lady Rhona." The Wolf Prince bowed regally. "By this time tomorrow, our alliance will be over, and the war will be won."

Rhona wiggled her fingers. "I could set fire to the castle from here, if you want it to be sooner. The walls are stone, but there is enough timber in there to burn."

His eyes widened in horror. "You cannot! Portia is in there, you said. Safe. You can't risk…and what of your man? The bargain we made? If he is dead, then he is freed of his vows, and I release you from yours."

Oh, the bitter gall, that both Portia and Grieve lived, and neither she nor Rudolf would be reunited with the ones they loved, for the pair no longer loved them. She had killed plenty of men, but she would not be the one to rip Rudolf's beating heart from his chest.

"He lives, too," Rhona said shortly. "Until tomorrow, then, Wolf Prince."

Thirty-Nine

It was strange to have a tent to herself again, but Rhona lingered there as long as she dared the next morning. She toyed with the idea of avoiding the noon peace council, but in her heart she knew she could not.

The Wolf Prince believed the cowardly Albans would surrender Portia. If she was lucky, Grieve would be among the girl's honour guard. Rhona could remain in the background and watch unseen as she saw how things played out between Portia, Grieve and Rudolf.

But when the boat landed, there were three armoured men aboard – no women.

Rudolf appeared as impassive as ever, not showing the surprise Rhona knew he must feel at not seeing Portia with them.

They came ashore, removing their helms as Rudolf did. That's when Rhona clapped both hands to her mouth to stifle her cry. The cowardly Albans had sent Grieve to treat with Rudolf in their place, without Portia. They'd sent him to his death.

Rhona had chosen a place where she could not hear them, and no magical breeze would carry their words across the whispering of half an army. She began to shove her way through the men, intent on hearing what was said. Grieve's last words, if that's what they were.

She would not let them be, she vowed. Even if he now loved Portia instead of her, she would not let him die.

A sword scraped out of its scabbard and Rhona lost patience. She sank her teeth into her lip, and magic blew a path for her to the lakeshore.

"Sheath that thing, you bloody fool!" she

shouted, running toward Grieve.

His eyes widened. "Rhona?" Down came the sword, and his eyes lit up.

Rhona could feel the fire inside her, ready to burn the world twice over in Grieve's defence. Thrice, if he loved her still.

"You lay one finger on this man, Wolf Prince, and our alliance is over!" She marched past Rudolf and took her place at Grieve's side. No man in Rudolf's army would rise in his defence against her.

Even Rudolf hesitated. He looked at Grieve for what was likely the first time. "Who are you?"

Before Grieve could speak, Rhona snapped, "He's Grieve Lewisson, my betrothed, and the head of Lady Portia's personal guard." She half expected him to wince at her words, but Grieve merely nodded. Rhona turned to Grieve. "Why have the Albans sent you to negotiate?"

The men behind Grieve burst out laughing. "What Albans? They've all fled, like the cowards they are. Even Mason, when we shut him out. Council Island and the castle belong to Lady Portia."

"No. It belongs to my husband."

Everyone turned to stare at the newcomer. Her red hair was a banner of flame brighter than anything Rhona could conjure, marking her as the lady herself. But as she approached, Rhona found it hard not to laugh. The third Little Pig indeed, for Lady Portia's gown was caked in mud to the knees.

Then Rudolf's eyes lit up, brighter than her hair. He mustn't have noticed the soiled gown as his oh-so-majestic lady made her muddy way along the lakeshore. He'd gone to war for her. Men had died for her. More men would die for her, if this war went on. One muddy girl.

A girl who hid behind her guards, and Grieve. No longer. Rhona fixed her gaze on the girl, willing her to show some sign of why they had all fought so long and so hard.

"My husband." When Portia repeated the words, she laid her hand on Rudolf's arm. She'd placed herself opposite Rhona, so that their eyes met.

Rhona expected curiosity, or

hostility…something that told her Portia had no idea who she was facing.

But Portia's face lit with a friendly smile. "Lady Rhona." Then she offered her cheek.

But she did not leave Rudolf's side or take her hand from his arm, all the while her gaze held Rhona's. In order to give Portia the kiss of peace custom demanded, Rhona would have to approach and bow her head to kiss the shorter girl.

Portia knew nothing about Rhona. Not her power or her rank or…anything. Every man present feared her, holding their breath as they waited to see Rhona's response, yet Portia smiled on, oblivious.

"It is a pleasure. I have heard so much about you," Portia said, glancing at Grieve.

Or not oblivious.

With one glance, she said it all. She knew all about Rhona's magic, for Grieve had told her, but she was Lord Angus's daughter. A politician, like her father before her. In her father's absence, Portia stood as ruler of the Isles, but she recognised Rhona's power over Rudolf's army. Between them, they held the power to end this war, unite everyone present, and bring peace.

Rhona would drop to her knees and kiss a pig for that. But Portia was no pig. She was a lady who outranked Rhona. A lady who winked, the moment Rhona's lips left her cheek, as though they were the best of friends sharing a secret.

They had done what countless fighting men could not do. Two women had ended a war with a kiss.

"I look forward to your wedding. You must sit beside me at the feast to celebrate mine. Of course, you and Grieve must sit with us at the high table. I insist." Portia's eyes were on Grieve as she said this. Either she enjoyed his pain or…was there nothing between her and Grieve, after all?

Rhona dared to hope.

"My lady," Grieve breathed. It wasn't clear which lady he was speaking to, as his eyes darted from one to the other.

Portia lifted her eyebrows. "I hope you mean Rhona, for I'm not yours any more. Protecting me is Prince Rudolf's job now."

Of course. Her marriage released him from his vows. Grieve was free.

Portia lifted her and Rudolf's linked arms, raising her voice in a warcry that would have made any general proud. "Isla is ours!"

The army – her army – echoed her words, over and over until the valley rang with a woman's warcry. As it should be.

Rhona felt a timid tap on her shoulder.

Grieve stood there, the only man among them not cheering. "I am no longer needed. Is there any chance…would you still be willing…I mean…"

"You'll marry me today, or not at all, Grieve Lewisson. I've waited long enough, and there's a priest hereabouts who will say the words for us, or I'll light his boots on fire," Rhona said.

"But what will your father say?" Grieve asked.

"Who cares, as long as you say yes?"

Of all the men present, Grieve alone had the power to crush Rhona entirely.

She moistened her lips. "If you don't say yes, I give you fair warning I'll light your boots on fire. I'm getting really good at that."

Grieve laughed. "You need no magic to light me on fire, my lady. But you have always known that. If you wish to be married today, then I will do everything in my power to grant your wish. The war is over. It is past time that you are wed."

"You're telling me." Rhona would have said more, but Grieve caught her in his arms, and her mouth was soon too busy for anything as dull as words.

Forty

Father Fintan was only too happy to perform the ceremony, boasting that he'd officiated in the prince's wedding to Portia, only last night. When Rhona finally said the words that she'd dreamed about for so long, she wasn't sure who was happier – her or Grieve. The priest pronounced them husband and wife, then dropped his voice to a whisper to tell Rhona he would happily counsel her on the duties of marriage at any time, especially after the wedding night.

Rhona just laughed. "If my husband has

forgotten how to please me in bed, I'm not the one you'll hear it from, Father. I'm not sure Grieve will confess it to you, either." She seized Grieve's hand. "Come, husband, we have a wedding feast to attend."

The camp was strangely empty, though the tents crouched like ghosts in the moonlight. Everyone else was in the castle, and the sounds of merry feasting carried across the water without the help of a breeze, magical or otherwise.

"The only feast I want is you." Grieve's words hung in the air, tantalising, tempting. Too much to refuse.

He tugged her into his arms. His embrace and the kiss that followed felt as natural as breathing – all things she wanted to do for the rest of her life.

"To my tent, then," she said, leading the way. She entered, waving her hand to light the braziers that turned the tent from chilly to bearable. She heard a clink behind her. Grieve's sword belt, most likely. He would not need it here.

"I have some wine here somewhere. It is

not a bottle of Father's best, but…"

"Perhaps after, my lady. I am drunk on you already."

No one spoke to her as sweetly as Grieve. Oh, how she'd missed that. Rhona whirled, wanting to see the love in his eyes as he looked at her.

He tugged off his hose and stood naked in the firelight. Her husband. War had only improved him, turning lean, boyish muscle into the harder, muscled man before her. Everything she could ever want.

Grieve laughed. "I seem to remember I was the one lost for words, seeing you naked. Have the tables turned?"

"I…" The fire began in her belly, coursing through her veins until it flamed in her cheeks. She'd never needed a man more than she wanted Grieve now. "I need to feel you inside me, Grieve. Now."

"Then let's get you out of this gown, for I've dreamed of you every night since the day I left." His hands didn't fumble as he unlaced her gown and had her out of it before he'd finished kissing her. Her shift vanished, and now she was naked before him. He carried her to the bed, fingers caressing her even as he kissed her. There was none of the boyish nervousness from before. Now, he played her body with the deft strokes of a masterful man.

Rhona arched her back as she cried out for joy, begging for more. Grieve had anticipated her, once again, thrusting deep into her before her first blissful orgasm had finished. On the second thrust, her hips rose to meet him, ever equal to anything he was willing to give.

They moved together, one body in more than mere words, until they uttered twin cries of joy as they reached their peak together, too.

It wasn't until they lay tangled in each other's arms later, that Rhona thought to say, "Remember that witch on Nimbanmore Isle? She would be horrified at what we've just done. She thought we were brother and sister, remember."

Grieve traced a circles around her nipples, grinning as she shivered at his touch. "There's only one witch whose opinion I care for. My lovely Lady Rhona, you never did tell me…what sort of lover am I?"

Her hands slid down his belly, stroking him into readiness. Only then did Rhona flash him a wicked smile. "I'm sure I've forgotten. But I'd love to be reminded."

Grieve rolled over, settling between her thighs. "What sort?" he demanded.

"One who likes to tease me," she grumbled, reaching for him.

He leaned forward and kissed her breasts. "If you will not say, then I will tell you. I am the sort of lover who will love you with every breath until the day I die. The sort who wants to hear my name on your lips as you cry out for pleasure, over and over again." He thrust into her, as if to punctuate his words. "And what sort of lover are you?"

She couldn't think, too intent on the pleasure of feeling the heat of him inside her again. Deep inside, where he belonged. "I'm yours," she said simply. "And as long as we're together, we get to live happily ever af….oh, Grieve!"

Grieve chuckled. "As my lady wishes, of course."

Forty-One

Briska stamped out of her boots, but the blazing leather had already set the floor alight. Swearing, she bit down hard and fought to cast the only spell that could save her. The circle of blue light flared and died, once, twice…but on the third time it seemed to stay, wavering a little, but enough. She stepped through the portal, which collapsed behind her. She peeled off her singed stockings, to find her feet red and blistered with burns. She stuck her feet in the water bucket, moaning as the icy water numbed the pain.

The mirror unclouded for a moment and a face appeared. "Well done," the woman said.

"What do you mean, well done? That brother and sister almost killed me!" Briska snapped.

The woman laughed. "Brother and sister? You are too easily persuaded. That's what got you into this mess in the first place, but I will help you. This pair are matched, and so you will move onto your next quest. Your new assignment is in the icy north, I'm afraid. You will need warmer things."

Ice and snow? Perfect for burned feet.

Briska lifted her arms. "I am ready when you are, Mistress." The last word came hard for a woman who had once been a queen, but she had little choice now. Slavery to the mirror and its mistress was all her life held now.

A portal opened before her, and Briska stepped through. The mirror, her chest of belongings, and her precious sack of spices landed in the snow behind her.

Another day, another couple. Though she shook her head when she thought of Hansel and Gretel. That pair would not have an easy time of it, she was certain. She might have made a match of them, however unwillingly, but they had a lot of work for even a hope of happily ever after.

Her mistress's face appeared in the mirror. "Next, you must match Kai and Gerda," she said.

Briska sighed as she saw the picture of the pair. At least these two had clothes on, unlike the fornicating brother and sister. Thank the heavens for small mercies. And snow to cool her feet.

From queen of a kingdom to queen of the snow, Briska's work was never done.

But first, she would need a place to live, for her new palace was gone. And all the ice and snow gave her an idea…

About the Author

Demelza Carlton has always loved the ocean, but on her first snorkelling trip she found she was afraid of fish.

She has since swum with sea lions, sharks and sea cucumbers and stood on spray drenched cliffs over a seething sea as a seven-metre cyclonic swell surged in, shattering a shipwreck below.

Demelza now lives in Perth, Western Australia, the shark attack capital of the world.

The *Ocean's Gift* series was her first foray into fiction, followed by her suspense thriller *Nightmares* trilogy. She swears the *Mel Goes to Hell* series ambushed her on a crowded train and wouldn't leave her alone.

Want to know more? You can follow Demelza on Facebook, Twitter, YouTube or her website, Demelza Carlton's Place at:

www.demelzacarlton.com

Books by Demelza Carlton

Ocean's Gift series
Ocean's Gift (#1)
Ocean's Infiltrator (#2)
Ocean's Depths (#3)
Water and Fire

Turbulence and Triumph series
Ocean's Justice (#1)
Ocean's Trial (#2)
Ocean's Triumph (#3)
Ocean's Ride (#4)
Ocean's Cage (#5)
Ocean's Birth (#6)
How To Catch Crabs

Nightmares Trilogy
Nightmares of Caitlin Lockyer (#1)
Necessary Evil of Nathan Miller (#2)
Afterlife of Alana Miller (#3)

The Complex series
Halcyon
Fishtail

Mel Goes to Hell series

Welcome to Hell (#1)
See You in Hell (#2)
Mel Goes to Hell (#3)
To Hell and Back (#4)
The Holiday From Hell (#5)
All Hell Breaks Loose (#6)

Romance Island Resort series

Maid for the Rock Star (#1)
The Rock Star's Email Order Bride (#2)
The Rock Star's Virginity (#3)
The Rock Star and the Billionaire (#4)
The Rock Star Wants A Wife (#5)
The Rock Star's Wedding (#6)
Maid for the South Pole (#7)
Jailbird Bride (#8)

Romance a Medieval Fairytale series

Enchant: Beauty and the Beast Retold
Dance: Cinderella Retold
Fly: Goose Girl Retold
Revel: Twelve Dancing Princesses Retold
Silence: Little Mermaid Retold
Awaken: Sleeping Beauty Retold
Embellish: Brave Little Tailor Retold
Appease: Princess and the Pea Retold
Blow: Three Little Pigs Retold
Return: Hansel and Gretel Retold
Wish: Aladdin Retold